THE STRAY

JASON M. FORD

De Novo Press

Nashville

The Stray

For information contact :

HTTPS://WWW.DENOVO.PRESS

Write to us at:

P.O Box 325
Nashville, TN 37076

If you've enjoyed the book, please leave a review!

Cover design by Zac Caffrey
Book layout by De Novo Press

ISBN: 978-1-7330817-0-2

Library of Congress Control Number: 2020933386

First Edition: March 2020

1 2 3 4 5 6 7 8 9 10

FOREWORD

Dear Reader,

I wracked my brain for what seemed like ages to write a forward that I felt was worth representing the first book published by De Novo Press, The Stray.

I was trying to come up with something that was poised and erudite, as we've come to expect from these types of things. I am the individual representing this new endeavor after all!

Let's be real, that's not what I or De Novo Press is all about, though.

At De Novo Press, we're dedicated to finding the best stories written by people just like you and bringing them to a wider audience. We believe everyone has a story to tell, just as we all love to hear the stories of others.

I started reading stories on Reddit, fanfic sites, and other digital platforms years ago and found that I was as engrossed and held captive by those stories as I was by some famous works by well-known authors. I became hooked and binged serials and desperately waited for new works to come out.

Realizing that there were countless great stories that only a relative few would get to read bummed me out. Bartenders, retail and office workers, teachers, students, and other everyday people write great stories every day. However, they don't see themselves as 'authors.'

De Novo Press is here to change that.

I created De Novo Press as a way to share those stories and prove to everyone you didn't have to be famous to get your stories out there.

I sincerely hope you enjoy reading The Stray as much as we enjoyed working on it. This was a work of love and learning and we look forward to sharing this story with the world.

A big 'Thank You' to those contributors who directly worked on this project and to all of the friends of De Novo

Press for your encouragement.

If you enjoy The Stray, please help support us and our authors by leaving a review on the many platforms and sharing
it with friends!

A sincere thank you for purchasing our book and we look
forward to bringing you more!

Marc Cox
Founder of De Novo Press

*P.S. Remember aspiring Authors, all famous writers started From
the Beginning!*

"Did I request thee, Maker, from my Clay
To mould me Man, did I sollicite thee
From darkness to promote me, or here place
In this delicious Garden?"

John Milton, Paradise Lost, 1667

THE STRAY

CHAPTER ONE
Homeless Pt. I

Light, again.

Ethan stirred beneath the cool sheets, drawing in the morning air deeply. There was an aroma so strong that he thought she must have been cooking in the bedroom. Bacon and pancakes? Sausage and eggs? He couldn't make out what it was, but it yanked his feet over the edge of the bed and sat him up.

He felt the warm hand of sunlight across his shoulders, prompting him to twist and look at the beautiful dawn which cast such long shadows. He walked across the old, hardwood floor which was cold beneath his feet, put on warm slippers and looked up into a round mirror on the wooden wall. Short black hair and brown eyes filled the reflection, which paused to check the length of the rough stubble on its chin. Ethan opened the door and stepped out of the room, still in his boxers and t-shirt.

Ethan walked through a short hallway to a spiral staircase

and descended to the first floor of the big, open house. The south and west walls had giant windows that stretched from the floor to the roof, looking out on the breathtaking alpine landscape which was enraptured in the morning light; the view was so clear that it may have been painted onto the glass. The house was styled as a log cabin made entirely of caramel, comforting wood. An enormous stone fireplace split the south wall down the middle, warming a sunken living area. Halfway down the stairs, he stopped abruptly to avoid a mug and saucer placed on the last of the black, cast iron steps. He picked up the white porcelain, drawing the fleeting steam into his nose.

v. 1. Have a desire to possess or do (something); wish for.

Reaching the bottom floor, he headed around the edge of the concave living room and walked around a few potted plants that hung from the wooden ceiling high above. His slippers scuffed across a large rug that accommodated the antique dinner table, finally bringing him to the large kitchen opposite the fireplace and the giant windows of the south wall. It had stone pillars, oak countertops, and a dirty blonde, golden, smiling woman with a frying pan of bacon.

"What a good morning," Ethan yawned, taking a seat on a stool by the kitchen island.

"You found your coffee," replied Cameron, sliding the breakfast meat onto their two plates with her spatula.

Ethan felt his stomach growling, muted by the sizzling. "You didn't step on it!" she added, plopping a fried egg in front of him with a pronounced smack. They laughed through a groggy telepathy.

They ate a quiet breakfast in the kitchen. Ethan kept looking around the scene, a playwright sitting in the aisle of his own sold-out show, appreciating it all. "What a good life," he thought to himself.

"So," said Cameron halfway through a piece of brown, buttered toast, "what plans do we have for today?"

"We should take the jeep down the mountain; look around town for a bit."

"Mmmm," Cameron replied. "And we can go fishing after that!"

"The lake or the river?"

"I think I'm in a lake mood today."

"Oh, that's too bad, because I'm definitely in a river mood."

Cameron held her chin for a second. "How about where the river meets the lake?"

Ethan smiled. "My favorite."

They gathered their fishing gear and headed out the front door. Walking across gravel they came to a beat up, old, yellow jeep. A grey dog trotted up behind Ethan. He knelt down to pet him, asking the King of the Mountain how his morning was. Cameron was already relaxing in the jeep, wearing a pair of sunglasses. Gracefully, her reclined body seemed to reflect the sunlight.

The old engine started up immediately and they were off. The driveway was long and narrow, with pine trees on the right and an overgrown field on the left behind a rusty pole-and- wire fence. They reached a paved road and headed towards town, breezing through patches of forest darkness and rock faces. The speedometer in the jeep was broken, but it didn't matter.

They came to a stretch of road that led along a cliff. On the other side of a guardrail, hundreds of feet below them, a calm river shone in the sunlight. Thousands of pine trees painted the spring canvas green with a few scattered, white clouds floating in the otherwise unblemished sky. The air was fresh and cooled their sun-warmed arms. Ethan looked over and poked Cameron, suspicious that she had fallen asleep. She lifted her shades and grinned, the wind blowing strands of hair across her white teeth.

The road continued to wind down the mountain, causing

them both to yawn forcefully as their ears popped.

"That's it!" cried Cameron, "I've had enough ear popping! We have to move!"

They both laughed.

CHAPTER TWO
Linear

Alarm set, alarm set quiet.

Eight o'clock. Ethan rose from his bed, his feet landing on warm carpet. He ate a cold bagel, checked the news and took the grey cement stairs to the parking garage. At work, he clocked in and the system began counting hours. After eight hours had passed, he clocked out and returned to his apartment, ascending to the third floor.

Hot shower.

Media.

Stir-fry.

Alarm set.

Repeat.

CHAPTER THREE
The Experiment

"Ethan, I think you're being too sensitive," said Alice. She had her hands out in front of her, balled up as little fists in subtle frustration. "Every single person here has the exact same devices. You'll forget they're there."

"That doesn't make it alright automatically," replied Ethan. "I can't get used to it."

Alice simply said, "Okay," and walked off with her knuckles still clenched.

Ethan had just received basic surgery to install electronic implants into his brain and index finger. Little circle chips with tendrils that reached out to envelope his nerve endings.

He worked at a water recycling plant in Philadelphia and they would help him when operating the facility's systems; however, he felt those tentacles engulfing his autonomy in a way. His brain had a new roommate, the very same one, it felt to him, as everyone else he knew. He finally relented, being the last employee at the plant to have them.

There was every reason for these implements to appear; workplace security and integration was only natural. More than that, however, was capital. The world had always been governed by the most basic laws of economics; now, those laws could be embedded even closer to that which governed them: the human. This had always been inevitable.

Ethan looked up from his desk to see Will approaching at a 9:00 AM pace, coffee in hand.

"How's it, today?" he asked.

"Nice and crisp. Doesn't taste polluted." Will looked about, replying, "Do you think there must be someone doing some work around here?"

He raised an eyebrow at Ethan, now. "Hey, you finally got implants, didn't you?"

"Yeah," Ethan replied with a tone of resignation.

Will snorted, putting on an inflated grin. "Well it's not 2020 anymore, Ethan. Times change!"

"Return Reynold's message, yet?" asked Ethan, changing the subject.

"Oh! Right" replied Will as he took a small grey pad out of his shirt pocket. The implant in his finger detected the device and automatically linked to it, connecting it with the implants in his brain.

He began speaking out a reply message in his head which was picked up and typed out onto the pad's small screen. "Thanks for reminding me," he said. "Oh! Get that message from the Science Institute?"

"I don't know, I haven't checked," replied Ethan, avoiding Will's expectant gaze. He would have to do it eventually, either voluntarily or after breaking under Will's frequent goading. He opened a desk drawer and produced his own pad.

Will was pleased. "Now just touch it with your implant and think, 'open new mail.'"

Ethan suddenly saw a new message on the screen. "Wow, its fast," he said as he began reading it. It was an invitation to take part in a survey and to be the subject of a month long experiment.

He looked up at his friend with a smirk. "So why does that seem to be the most exciting thing to you all week?"

"Wouldn't it be nice to have a month long vacation?"

"Vacation from what?" asked Ethan.

Will sighed. "It would be nice to get out of this for a month. I've been doing the same thing every day of my life for the past five years. Not one vacation – paid or otherwise."

"Well I can say the same; I mean not many people at all go on vacations anymore." Will replied, "Those people don't work here. I think you could really use it. Let's both do it."

Ethan leaned back in his chair, smiling to himself. "I don't know, Will."

"I'm doing the survey. I'm applying for the experiment. Then I'm doing it again under your name - but relax, it's not like you'll be picked."

Ethan laughed. He knew it was useless to resist; he might as well just fill it out. "Maybe I'll get around to it," he muttered to himself.

The chilly morning air did not feel refreshing to Ethan like usual. It instead seemed to meet him with an inconsiderate harshness as he travelled down the sidewalk, like a stranger who didn't bother to move out of his path. He was headed to the Science Institute of Philadelphia.

He had finished the survey haphazardly. It was easy

enough, especially with his new implants (a fact he bitterly admitted to himself). It seemed to predominantly inquire about his sleep habits, such as how many hours per night he slept, or the number of dreams he could usually remember upon waking.

Nearing his destination, the air swirled about him together with a soundscape of quiet, efficient vehicles and artificial voices. He could barely remember how a normal internal combustion engine sounded, though it had been a matter of only a few years since air-cleansing cars - some new models and some converted from gasoline to carbon intake - had completely taken over. Government subsidy programs had been introduced abruptly at the expense of the taxpayer. Motorists scowled at shrunken paychecks and honked their horns which were a welcome, familiar sound occasionally heard over the strange, low buzzing of their altered engines. The carbon cars gave the city environment a false aura of sedation, a change which was only one out of very many that gave the world a new, placated face. Ethan felt as if he had once lived in another era.

"Hello," said the receptionist as Ethan entered the Science Institute.

"Hi, I'm Ethan. Ethan Walter."

"Oh! Professor Holtz will want to see you right away," she said, directing him to the Professor's office and opening the door.

"Professor," she said in a sing song voice, "Ethan Walter is here!" Ethan entered quietly.

"Ah, welcome," said the Professor. "I'm Jared Holtz and this is my partner, Alexander Spurlock. Please have a seat, Ethan! We have... quite the proposition for you."

Ethan shook their hands and seated himself while quickly looking about the office. He was immediately met with the impression that Holtz was a professor of great prestige. His office was well decorated with grandiose awards and photos of Holtz with prominent political figures. The Professor himself was unimposing, with kind eyes behind thick glasses and a relaxed smile carrying a white mustache.

"You've been selected as the subject of our experiment!" said Professor Holtz. "Congratulations!"

"Thank you," Ethan replied. Ethan had suspected as much. He tried to seem excited, but he realized the futility in the attempt as he spoke the words. As a result, a crooked smirk came onto his face. He suddenly became quite angry at Will. He couldn't believe he had actually been selected.

"You don't sound very thrilled," observed Professor Holtz. He glanced over at his partner.

"This experiment is a very noteworthy endeavor in the scientific community," said Spurlock. "It's set to be somewhat of a milestone. Professor Holtz has been working towards it for the past two years."

Ethan nodded and touched his chin, trying not to be disrespectful. He planned on turning the offer down and getting back to routine life.

"And of course you will be paid handsomely," said Spurlock. Ethan's eyebrows jumped to attention by themselves. "Two-thousand dollars per day."

"After taxes?" asked Ethan, his false interest suddenly infused with sincerity.

"After taxes!" replied Professor Holtz. He was sharp and observant, and could see that Ethan was ready to hear about the experiment. "You'll be staying in an enclosed environment for 30 days. Because of the nature of what we're studying, we've fitted a normal house with the equipment we'll need. All you will be required to do is eat, sleep, and relax."

"That's all? I'm just going to be living in a home for a month?" asked Ethan in amusement.

"Yes! The important work will be done as you sleep."

Holtz motioned towards Ethan's shirt pocket. "See that pad you have?"

"It basically reads my mind."

"That's exactly right. It connects to the implant in your finger, which talks to the implant in your head. That implant then taps into the part of your brain that controls speaking, and literally snatches the words right out of your mouth! The things we've learned in the past few years which allowed us to do that are making it possible to do even more." Holtz paused to allow an almost childish grin. "We're going to see your dreams!"

Ethan was visibly perplexed. "For the 30 days you'll be living in the experiment home, whenever you sleep, we'll be recording what you dream!"

Spurlock piped in, raising a finger. "Actually, not everything. Only the strongest dreams. Only the dreams about things – people – that are already rooted in your memory."

"Oh, right!" replied Holtz. "He's right, only the dreams that are most coherent and connected to things for which you already have a certain amount of information in your brain."

"You'll be recording them so you can play them back on a monitor or something?" Ethan asked.

"A projector, actually."

"What are you trying to find out? Are you just testing out the technology?"

"This is an experiment that will lead to so very many discoveries. We'll be testing all sorts of things, not simply the equipment."

For the first time, Ethan was intrigued by this new opportunity. He sat in thought for a few moments, trying to envision what the 30 days would be like.

"Questions?" asked the intuitive Professor.

"Yes," replied Ethan, foreseeing an immediate issue. "What if I said I don't usually dream very much?"

"Oh, but you do!" replied Holtz, his teeth showing again, lifting his mustache. "You dream throughout the night. Everyone does! You simply don't remember the dreams when you awake."

"I suppose I won't have to, once the experiment begins!" "You are correct. The things in your dreams will be very, very real to you. Have you ever heard of a neutrino projector? No? Allow me to explain."

CHAPTER FOUR

The Game

Footsteps on leaf-littered sidewalk came to Ethan's ears as a very clear whisper. Just beyond, the concrete turned to asphalt, on which electrics almost seemed to float by. Across the asphalt, grass marked the edge of a park. A group of kids were playing a game of baseball. Ethan watched as the boy on first stole second behind the pitcher's back, who threw a fastball, striking the batter out.

Ethan looked up at a waitress standing beside his table. "More coffee?" she asked. Ethan shook his head, smiling politely. He was at the café at the corner of his apartment building. This is where he usually chose to relax when the weather was nice, and fall weather was his favorite.

He happened to be sitting now where he had sat with his girlfriend almost a year prior. It was the day they had parted ways. The sounds of the sidewalk, the street, and the park moved to the back of Ethan's mind as he recalled their conversation.

"When was that?" she asked, her hand moving to her forehead.

Ethan replied, "After we got back from the day at the museum. I remember it very clearly, Cameron."

"I said, 'I want us to go further?'"

"Yes," said Ethan, "It wasn't even a month ago. Please just relax, and remember that we're both adults, now. We're not going to go off on a whim every day and fool around. We should make better use of our time."

"You're making it into something else. That's an exaggeration," retorted Cameron.

Ethan looked out across the street at the snow-covered park. The benches and trash bins poked out above the white, pure landscape. "I think you're exaggerating, too."

n. 1. A line or border separating two countries.

Cameron leaned forward, an amused smirk peering over the top of her big scarf. "Oh really?" she replied. Her voice was intoned with a masked pain that contrasted her expression. "All you do, Ethan, is go to work every morning and stay in every night. I used to be the same way and that's why we got along fine for the past two years. But I got sick of it and finally got myself moving again..."

"Reverted back a few years, you mean?" interrupted Ethan.

"And then," she continued assertively, her mask breaking, her mouth retreating below the edge of her scarf, "I tried to get you out of your shell. But I decided to give up! You're a part of my life that doesn't progress, and doesn't go forward, like things are supposed to go!" Her voice began to break, too. "It is absolutely through, Ethan. You can get back to your world and keep everything exactly the way it is, except me."

Ethan was surprised at her sudden surge of emotion.

15

He thought to himself, aren't I the one in a position to feel grief? "I don't understand how trying to be responsible and being able to pay the bills isn't a part of moving on, growing up!"

"Of course, everyone has to do it; it is part of growing up," she replied, "But you're stuck in a different way."

"That's a little vague."

"You stay exactly the same, every day. Things happen, time goes on, but you don't."

Ethan sighed and put up his hands. "So now you'll just pretend that you're changing your life, and everything is so much better, but you'll cry."

Her scarf caught her tears before they reached her neck. "I'll be different."

Ethan's attention returned to the game of baseball in the park, where spots of late sunlight cast golden tint on the tops of the trees and squirrels scampered about their dim trunks. Some of what she said was true, he thought to himself.

Ethan still couldn't believe it had actually happened; him! Out of the millions of candidates for the experiment, they picked him. He acknowledged that it was mostly a good thing, considering the hefty pay. He had forgotten his intense apprehension towards recent technology, however, until after leaving Professor Holtz's office.

So much had changed so fast. Renewable, dirt-cheap energy had abruptly been attained, and within a matter of years everything looked different. Limitations imposed by power requirements disappeared, opening a world of new possibilities. It was as if science was boosted up to a new level. Computers which had been top-of-the-line equipment sat collecting dust, replaced. Simple appliances such as refrigerators and microwaves began a mass migration from the kitchen to the street curb. Gas stations became empty lots on intersections all over the world.

It was all replaced by things that used to be ideals; objectifications of the most efficient, evolved facilities of everyday life. One of them had been installed directly into Ethan. His implants replaced his laptop computer and his phone, and then, as if using Ethan's body to finally eliminate an old nemesis, threw his calendar, pens, notepads, books, and wallet into the trash. He was left with a single, small grey pad. Those corner gas station burial grounds were filled with garage access points where one could park and then watch their automobiles descend below ground to be automatically stored and recalled within a moment's notice. Alternatively, they were also topped with "mediums," places where people could go to safely touch finger implants and communicate novels of thought without the need for words or voices. They were safe due to a regulatory system which was never seen or heard, yet trusted.

Most people welcomed the changes, but some opposed them. There were those who staged violent protests in the streets of Silicon Valley. This was the place that a journalist - beset by phenomenal stories of progress - pinned as the Tree of Life from which the knowledge came. The rest simply followed suit after their own searching for some sort of genesis ended fruitlessly. More commonly, people simply abstained – as much as was possible, anyway. To have done so fully would have meant a type of isolation. The steps between individual thought and some sort of collective communion were growing very few, and teetered on that little grey interface. It was the ticket back into the Garden.

Then there was Ethan. He wasn't necessarily opposed to it all; however, he couldn't help but feel in some way excluded. He felt his life had been on track. Then the entire world suddenly changed. It became necessary for him to get a carbon car, and a new work facility, and implants intruded into his body. The government didn't pass any laws requiring such changes but it became for all intents and purposes an unwritten commandment.

He was also afraid of the scientific implications. Man could now tap into the mind more deeply. The basic functions of the implants were just beginning. In LA there was a supercomputer that had recently been completed. It was the most advanced computer ever, being more powerful than its closest predecessor by a hundred fold. It had been turned on now for a year and it was undergoing an analysis of a human brain, mapping, analyzing, and cataloging every single neural connection. Ethan had to stop himself from thinking about what such an endeavor would mean. Before man would even reach Mars or cure global starvation or attain world peace he would enter a revelation so bright as to burn, to char into smoke with an aroma of humanity's sacrificed soul his opened skull - he would be able to map the individual. No thought would be without receipt, no emotion would have excuse, and no memory would be left to lie in its deep rest.

The possibilities that entered Ethan's mind as he let it wander on the subject seemed fantastic and impossible. But he knew with an ever-growing certainty that such was not the case – or wouldn't be for long. Uploading a person's mind, preserving it, would seem shockingly simple. Immortality would be realized, but in an almost absurdly unassuming actuality that strangled the ambitious, ancient concept with a cold functionality. An immortal race, living in circuits, introduced into the afterlife by a simple upload complete with a progress bar, a mockery. But would the end result really be the individual, or something else, something less?

Ethan rubbed his thumb and index finger together, feeling the implant under his skin. He looked up to see the game of baseball once more, and it offered his mind an elegant answer to such dark conjecture.

The ball flew through the crisp fall air, landing with a thud in an oversized catcher's mitt. It transferred to the player's other hand immediately and was launched again, being caught by the third baseman that jumped a bit to reach it. He came down just in time to catch the opposing player's sliding foot.

Human life, thought Ethan, was like a game. The player does not know what the outcome of the game will be. There are thousands of different possibilities posed by each pitch of the baseball, and each single action – influenced by the sequence of actions taken before it – alters the course of the game. Each player uses whatever information is available to him to make the best decisions and he tries to predict the next action that will be taken. But in the end, he can never know how the events will progress until they are decided; in fact, it would be pointless to play the game if he did.

Ethan recalled the last words Cameron ever spoke to him: 'I'll be different.' He almost said it out loud to himself. For the first time he fully understood why she left him. She was right. Every day of his life was a sequence of events, just as everyone else's; things happened, time went on; linear, human existence progressed; but he didn't play the game.

CHAPTER FIVE
Briefing

"I can't believe it," said Will, smiling wide and shaking his head.

"I'm astonished you didn't turn them down!"

Ethan shrugged. "They're paying me."

"Must be more pay than what we're getting here, huh?"

"Yeah," said Ethan. Will said nothing, a solid grin stubbornly stuck to his face.

"Two-thousand per day."

The grin flatlined, the life in Will's face ascending into his now bulging eyes. "After taxes?"

"That's right," replied Ethan, flattening his tie with his dimples showing.

Alice walked up to the two. She would often make trips around the office simply to reset her mental location, as she held the most technical position out of their team of three.

She appreciated what little entertainment Ethan and Will brought to the workplace - Ethan for his amusing neurotic episodes and Will for his near-mystifying thickness.

"Something exciting?" she asked.

Will replied, "Ethan's getting paid two-thousand dollars a day to be in that experiment!"

"You're joking!" she gasped, her chewing gum rolling to a stop at the bottom of her gaping mouth. "That's amazing news, Ethan! I noticed a headline about that on the feed the other day. It said the entire scientific community is watching it."

Ethan tried to underplay the significance of the headline, suddenly feeling uncomfortable with all the attention. "Well, these days a hundred amazing new experiments are going on at once. This experiment is just one more."

"Oh no, Ethan," she replied, "I thought that when I first read the headline, too, but I read the subtext, and it said that this one, in particular, was supposed to really be something."

Will spoke up. "For paying someone two-thousand dollars a day, it better be!"

"What do you have to do, anyway?" Alice asked, ignoring Will's benign submission. She was now chewing her gum in that slow, closed-mouth fashion of hers when she found a conversation worth her full attention.

"Well," said Ethan as he scratched his head, "pretty much nothing. I'm going to be living in a normal old house for 30 days, and they're going to be recording my dreams."

Will said, "You mean 'dream,' singular: big, fat check."

"Like writing them down as you describe them?" asked Alice.

Ethan realized this concept was indeed hard to grasp. "No," he replied. "It's extremely complicated. The Professor had to dumb it down a bit for me to understand. They'll record what's in my head when I dream. It's like how implants can detect what you're saying in your mind, but more advanced. Then they're going to recreate it."

Both were visibly perplexed. Alice asked, "but you feel you understand what they're going to do?"

"Yeah, just enough at least," Ethan replied.

"Enough to feel like you're up to something like that?" she asked. "I would have thought you of all people would think twice about having your mind read."

Ethan said, "I won't really have my mind read, just part of it. I know what you mean, but it's not as 'out there' as I probably made it sound."

"To be honest, you sound broke," Alice said, chewing her gum faster again.

"I –," Ethan cut himself short as the boss walked into the room. Will and Alice quietly dispersed.

The day went on. Ethan made his rounds. He was at his desk an hour before it came time to leave. He took out his small, grey interface pad and accessed his conversation with Professor Holtz when they had met in his office. His implants had automatically recorded everything and transcribed it into a text log. He began reading at the point where the conversation became both exciting and worrisome:

Ethan Walter > They won't be just holograms?

Jared Holtz > No, they'll be physical reproductions, anatomically correct right down to the marrow.

Ethan Walter > So they'll be clones?

Jared Holtz > No. As I said, they will be projected. So in that sense, they will be somewhat like a hologram. They won't be organically grown or assembled, because the neutrino projector will make them exist, will hold them together.

Ethan Walter > How will it know to make their bodies accurate? I suppose I can understand their faces, it can see them like looking at a photograph.

Alexander Spurlock > No, you've got it wrong, there. What is the act of seeing? Your eyes are a tool, they directly detect photons. Without a sufficient number of photons active in a room your eyes do not work. This AI is in no way as limited as that.

Ethan Walter > But what about things like, I don't know, birthmarks? How it will know to recreate things like that?

Jared Holtz > Remember, we'll only be using the most vivid dreams, with persons and things that you know enough about. It is just using information from you; all data it uses to create anything will be solely from your mind. Whatever you know about them, it will know to recreate.

n. 1. The combination of characteristics or qualities that form an individual's distinctive character.

Ethan Walter > Well... what will they do?

Jared Holtz > The reproductions? They'll behave exactly like they would in real life - or rather as their real counterparts, originals would, actually. How you knew them to act, how you will dream that they move. It's really the same procedure as when it creates their physical body; in fact, the same. The body - the brain - of the reproduction will be the source of the recreated personality, the recreated individual... I suppose this is still confusing.

Ethan Walter > Yeah.

Jared Holtz > Think of it like this: we evolved, act, and think the way we do because of evolution, because of the laws of physics, yes?

Ethan Walter > Yes, I guess that must be true.

Jared Holtz > Right. Well imagine that we've found a tool with which to direct those rules. The reproductions' own brains and bodies must follow them, but we can create them

- their personalities, bodies, and idiosyncrasies, all based on information about them that you possess.

Ethan Walter > Mmm.

Alexander Spurlock > Ethan, what the professor is trying to say is that the reproduction is more like a marionette than an average person, except that a string is attached to every single atom. As he said, it is a physical body just like mine or yours; its vital functions will be primarily running; however, everything it does - essential functions included - only takes place because the projector manipulates the matter. Everything the reproduction says will be taking place because the projector will move its diaphragm, esophagus, tongue, lips, facial tissues, throat muscles, etcetera, molecule by molecule.

Ethan Walter > It will be contracting all the muscles?

Alexander Spurlock > Mmm, no, but you're getting close. It will forego that and just move the material by itself, because it's holding the stuff there in the first place. Really, this is all a bit unnecessary to explain. The outcome of the experiment won't be altered by whether you understand how it works. Actually, I think it better that you don't.

Jared Holtz > Ethan, look at it like this. Picture a standard, old-fashioned projector playing a video recording of a man. Now imagine that man turned into flesh and blood, like you and I. He still only moves and speaks as the projector shoots out the information. The light it projects is replaced with matter. It still dictates every single nuance that you perceive, and it knows how to do it because of the tape that someone put into it to play. Except in our case, the tape is replaced by the most advanced artificial intelligence ever, using data solely fed to it from your dreams, and memory - your perception. Does that make better sense?

Ethan Walter > Yes, actually. But instead of being projected onto the wall, it's here in three dimensions, just like us.

Alexander Spurlock > Yes, that's right.

Jared Holtz > Exactly. And it's very intricate, as we are an anatomically correct model, and it's made from the same stuff as you and I.

Ethan put the pad away. Reading over the attempts of Spurlock and Holtz to explain the experiment helped him to understand it a little more clearly, but he knew there was still an element that he couldn't work out. He quietly waited for the last few minutes at his desk and clocked out.

Ethan tried to predict what his stay in the house would be. It was a preoccupation which had invaded his mind ever since he left the Science Institute. He realized how frightened he was. It wasn't just the thought of scientists probing deep into his mind; it was the idea of meeting these fake people, these reproductions. He couldn't possibly imagine what it would be like to meet something that was merely imitating someone he knew. He realized he would necessarily be meeting with a personification of a computer program. He became confident it would be a dreadful experience.

When he arrived home, he searched for more information about the "neutrino projector" that Professor Holtz talked referenced. He found a page which tried to explain it basically:

"The neutrino projector is an instrument that possesses great potential, both in scientific and practical ways. It is the first instrument designed to control matter on a subatomic level remotely, and it has so far proven itself to be a resounding success. With this apparatus, one can virtually create anything, thanks to the research of NeuroTech Labs.

"The neutrino projector takes building materials (different kinds of molecules) that are in the surrounding environment – pre-supplied depending on the object you want to create – and forms them into structures. Because of recent discoveries we've made about neutrinos, we're able to use these particles to arrange molecules in incredible ways once thought impossible. The neutrino projector (which is a vast array of sensors as well as up to 500,000 separate projector modules) can use the neutrinos to recreate practically any biological structure in its exact, original, working form.

"All of this would be impossible if an immensely powerful computer didn't run it. Powerful processing is needed for the astronomically intricate calculations and precise measurements required to manipulate every molecule. If a supercomputer like this were shown to a scientist ten years ago, they would have insisted that it was from hundreds of years in the future – but we have it now!

"With this supercomputer analyzing every tiny particle in a given environment – which so far must be limited in size to about 20,000 cubic feet – it uses the neutrinos to compile a structure of molecules which is a virtually flawless recreation."

Ethan was reminded again of the supercomputer in LA. It was mapping out a human brain, the mass of many neuron connections that made a person who they were. What if a neutrino projector could build such a blueprint? According to the description Ethan read, it would be able to. Deep down it seemed inevitable.

Ethan felt the terrifying conclusion setting in. The projector could arrange matter and build synapses. But it could not inject the spark that would make the replica alive, could it? Could this really equate to creating life? His mind dug for rationalizations to blur the dark prophecy.

He put the pad away and let out a deep breath. It was getting late, and he was no more at peace than when he began reading. Maybe, he thought, he was foolish to think he could predict the future. But he also knew the strange future he had chosen, and the anxiety of knowing it would come.

The next meeting at the Science Institute was in a couple of days. He would be briefed on what exactly to expect of the experiment, and when it would get underway. Then, he would be going to sleep in a house surrounded by a tangle of Frankensteinian equipment and waking up every morning to face what was beginning to feel more and more to him like a fearful mystery, a residency with the unknowable.

Alarm set.

The next evening Ethan was reclined in his apartment, his arms stretched back behind his head, his socks wrinkled and drooping on his cold feet. He was staring at his muted holographic screen, which he had set to transmit to his implants. It was a first, for him, and he tried to breathe steadily as the media program monologued into his head.

Narrator> it is the concept that everything is already set in motion that every little thing which comprises our universe is following physical laws and that because of this there is only one physically possible universe

Narrator> the first published definition of causal determinism was in 1814 by the French mathematician Pierre-Simon Laplace it became known as Laplace's demon it stated that if one were to have complete knowledge of every particle in the universe according to Newtonian physics one would be capable of calculating their trajectories and would know the future just as the past

A pigeon landed on the small balcony outside. It instantly brought a fond memory into the front of Ethan's mind which cut through the telepathic program.

It was of a winter day five years ago. Ethan had been sitting out on the front porch of his parents' home in the country, talking with his father, Jack. He was a professor at the local university and had taught biology, physics, and mathematics. He was a lover of science, and as Ethan had watched him grow older, he noticed that his father's drive towards knowledge had only grown stronger.

Ethan remembered their talk very clearly.

"I almost was turned into an ice cube yesterday," said

Jack. He held up an invisible bean in front of his face. "This close."

"Oh yeah?" replied Ethan with a grin.

"I went jogging out on the trail along the river with Charlie. First time I've been down there since last spring. I had to pass that raised area by that big old fallen tree, and I almost lost my footing because of Charlie. He almost shoved me right off."

"I've come close to falling in at that point myself, without any help from Charlie," said Ethan.

Jack bent down and patted the dog's matted, grey shoulder. "I love animals."

"How's that?" asked Ethan. He had never known his father to be an outspoken animal lover.

"Because they know the secret to living." Jack replied.

"I wasn't aware there was such a secret!" Ethan chuckled.

Jack sighed, his eyes narrow. "I remember back when I was very young and swamped with homework. I would look at our dog Lem. He didn't have to do homework. He wasn't worried about a thing. It was a youthful whim at the time, but I was on to something."

Ethan asked, "Which was?"

"Well, I was right. Lem wasn't worried about stuff like that. It never entered his mind. Animals don't have the mental capacity or information that we do, but they don't need it. I think it would ruin them. They're each put together a certain way so that they function in their environment according to their physical abilities, right? It's real art in its most advanced form, I think. They don't have to consider living; they don't ask the question; in every single moment, they simply live."

Ethan was surprised to hear this from his father, a biologist of 20 years. He wasn't usually so sentimental. He replied, "But nature is full of chaos; it's overwhelming suffocation, not harmony."

"Of course. Catastrophes and tragedies occur every day in the natural world. But those tragedies are actually where it becomes even more admirable, in a sense. The animals fight to exist, to overwhelm as a species; to the last breath, they struggle towards their sole concern: to stay alive. Some animals fail, and their material is assimilated by the other life forms, and their life is thus sustained. It can sound cold and harsh, but really when I watch an animal, I know it isn't."

Ethan crossed his arms. "Why's that? How's it admirable?"

"Because with every single action – playing, running, killing, dying – they celebrate their existence. Really, watch an animal. Just sit and watch a cat playing with a string or whatever. It's worried about absolutely nothing; not the future, or homework, or the meaning behind things, or anything else."

"Well, that's because it CAN'T. It doesn't have the capacity to. It doesn't have a choice," said Ethan.

"But that doesn't take away the merit of it. We view that as a disadvantage to the cat. But the cat simply exists until it cannot, and in that ultimate fate – a fate we hold in common, you see – it is still celebrating an existence of something that is simply there, and doesn't ask for more than that."

Just then, a pigeon flew by. Jack pointed, saying, "There! That pigeon is demonstrating my point right now. It is endowed with an amazing ability of direction, which until recently even we didn't understand. But it is doing what it does to the best of its ability. It doesn't question it, and it celebrates it with every flap of its wings!"

"What is our ability?"

Ethan watched from his living room as the pigeon flew

away. He hadn't spoken to his father in months. He assumed they were doing alright back home, just as he was doing okay. The last message he got from them said everything was normal, except that Charlie had died. He felt a lump in his throat when he had read it, but at the same time remembered then, too, his talk that day with his father.

Suddenly, the program which had been transmitting to him cut back through his thoughts.

Narrator> the fact that in this model of our universe even the particles inside of our heads which constitute what we think feel say and do are also on such a trajectory set in motion 13.7 billion years ago and predetermined by the laws of physics

He turned off the program. He found himself in one final moment of doubt, considering if he should back out of the experiment. He then remembered Cameron's words to him in the park.

He was ready to play ball.

"Hello again, Mr. Walter!" said Professor Holtz, shaking Ethan's hand but with his interface pad still in his own, which fell to the ground. The Professor picked it up and gazed at the screen for a moment before seeming to suddenly remember Ethan was there, continuing, "Please allow me to introduce you to our team! Alexander Spurlock, as you already know." He pointed to the tall, lanky man with black hair and sneakers. Then he pointed to a very average looking college student with a clipboard. "That's Mario," he continued.

He pointed to and introduced everyone in the room. Ethan's head moved automatically from one to the next, nodding each time. He stopped trying to remember the names halfway through. The Professor finished, then noted, "There are a couple of interns that will also be participating, but they're not important."

Ethan nodded. "Good to meet you all."

"You must be excited," replied Mario. "Maybe a little anxious, too, huh?"

"Yes, both. I don't know what to expect."

"Ethan," said Professor Holtz, "I must admit, neither do we. I can assure you there's no harm in the experiment, and keep in mind that you can leave whenever you wish, without forfeiting any pay earned up to that point." He stopped there and eyed Ethan.

Even if he would be free to leave whenever, Ethan would never go back on a commitment. He seemed to look far into the distance for a few moments, and the room was silent. He stepped up to the plate. "Let's start!"

"Excellent! Please follow me to the lab!" said the Professor.

They left the Science Institute and walked along the sidewalk. Two blocks down Ethan could see a large, tan aluminum building on a fenced-in lot. It was a basic workshop style structure. From one block away he could see another building behind that was the same, but slightly smaller.

"That large building is the lab. It's full of very advanced technology. The smaller structure houses the power source for the neutrino projector. It's all fenced in and always locked up tight. We also have a guard on duty at all hours. The equipment attached to the house has to be watched over."

As they approached the front gate entrance, the house came into view from behind the lab. Ethan whistled and slowed his pace. It was an average looking house, painted a light yellow with maroon shutters. However, it was covered with large pieces of odd looking machinery. Along one of its sides was attached a metallic box at least 10 feet high with cones protruding out from it like the bottom of an egg carton. From each cone ran a vacuum tube that snaked its way across the outside of the house. Each tube disappeared into the structure at different places. One led right down through the shingles, another through the front wall next to the door. Hovering a few feet over the roof was a large black disk that was attached to a sort of rail system that encompassed the perimeter of the house. Other pieces of equipment of varying shapes and sizes were scattered about, all jutting from the walls and roof. The house almost looked like a magnet that had been dipped into a bucket of bolts and screws and then pulled out.

"Quite a sight, isn't it?" asked Holtz. "We usually keep it behind a barrier so that it doesn't attract too much attention, but we wanted you to see it."

"Why does it have to be a normal house like this? Couldn't you have simply made a model home inside of a real lab? Or at least picked a house that wasn't within the city limits?"

Holtz nodded. "We could have, but we decided it wasn't a concern. We don't want you to feel like a lab mouse or displaced. From inside the house, none of the equipment will be visible or audible."

"Will I be able to leave the house?" asked Ethan.

"Yes, but it is preferable that you don't. The neutrino projector will be scanning your mind at all times."

"What? How is that possible?"

"Quite easily," Holtz said. "It will be using the standard implants that are already in your brain to gather information. As soon as we turn it on it will acquire a connection with them..." He lectured on but Ethan could only think of the words, 'scanned at all times.' Maybe Alice had been right. He kept walking.

They entered the lab. It was one big room, filled with instruments and machinery. They sat around a table that was in the middle of it all.

The Professor stood and addressed the group. "Well, here we are. It's been a long couple of years preparing for this. We still don't know what we'll find in the end, but it's guaranteed to be something extraordinary.

"Today we're here for a briefing of the experiment. Everyone here has been involved for at least a year, except Mr. Walter. Thus, I won't extend a drawn out explanation. But first I must say thank you to Mr. Walter for choosing to be a part of this milestone endeavor."

"Glad to be of service," said Ethan, clumsily.

"The idea here is to study the response to stimuli. The subject will be shown incentives, and the computer will analyze his response. Not just his surface reactions, but everything that will be happening in his mind.

"The stimuli will be recreated persons from the subject's dreams, supplemented by his memory. Each night, Ethan will fall asleep, and the computer will gather the required data, and will use it to create a physical model in the house. The behavior of the reproduction will be an accurate representation of what the subject perceived it to be from interacting with the actual person in the past. This is where memory will come into play. We'll need his memories to fill in the gaps. We can't base the AI's behavior – or physical appearance – just from the subject's dreams.

"Then, upon waking, the subject will interact with the reproduction. At our first meeting, Mr. Walter had a bit of apprehension towards the idea, but we have a more in-depth explanation of the nature of the reproductions which abated his anxieties somewhat. I imagine there are still some, but I assure you now, Ethan, they are unfounded. You'll more than likely find the reproductions very pleasant, as they will essentially be the people you know and love the most."

Ethan found that last bit strangely unsettling, but hoped that maybe the Professor was right.

"At some point during each day, we will come into the

house and have a debriefing. We also have nanorecorders in every room. We'll ask you to keep a journal, and you'll also have a report sheet. You'll fill it out daily, and it will provide us with your interpretation of your feelings and reaction to the stimuli. After 30 days, we'll go over all the information in a debriefing, and once that's satisfied you'll receive your payment. You'll be done! The experiment will begin on Thursday morning at nine."

A question-and-answer period followed. Ethan had some questions. He wanted to know how often he could take a break away from the AI's probing; how long until the AI knew everything about him; where everything that the AI learned would end up. He gave everyone a friendly hand-shake before leaving. They all seemed more assured and at peace about the next month, but that didn't seem to rub off on him.

CHAPTER SIX

Promised

Cameron swept the covers aside.

"Hey!" cried Ethan.

"Oh stop it." She walked into the master bathroom, and Ethan heard the sink running. Lines of sunlight from the bed to the ceiling were cast upon the wall through the vertical blinds.

"Should we go to the museum?" she said, the voice reverberating.

"Definitely!" Ethan replied. His feet hit the carpet, and he slipped on a pair of socks. He fell backward onto the bed, staring up. Sunlight hit his right eye, so he closed it. "I'd hate to go through life without any depth perception."

"Yeah, me too," said Cameron.

He grinned. "I had an ex who was blind in one eye."

"Was it a shallow relationship?" She walked back into the

bedroom.

He said, "You know, Cameron, you're not just another girl to me."

"What am I?"

"Someone who thinks the same things that I do at the same time."

Cameron cocked her head. "Hhhmm, are you sure? Could I ever really know?"

"Well, no," Ethan answered, "But I just never thought anyone could be like that for me. I thought relationships weren't like that, I thought they were… less than that."

"Well, what exactly in the world did you think they were?" She asked.

"I don't know… transactions? Arrangements?" He felt the warmth on his right eyelid, the light cascading yellow over the tiny veins and creases like the colors and lines of a painting. "Inevitable."

"Maybe the only ones that work are the ones that nobody can control," submitted Cameron.

Ethan stood, gathering his pants and buttoning up. "That's counterintuitive, huh?"

She replied, "Intuition can be a powerful ally of illusion, right? Sometimes a person can have an illusion of control, maybe just because intuition seems to demand it. And what about when someone completely lacks intuition?"

"That reminds me of something about our first real date. I chickened out when it came time to make a move; you hugged me."

"And?"

He continued, "You held me so long it began to feel like, 'sorry.'"

"You lack intuition generally, I think," laughed Cameron.

"Well, I guess you're right. At the point when I felt like I lost all control, we went out again."

"Oh Ethan, guys need to be controlling and assertive, don't you know?"

He smirked and continued dressing. "We should get going, it'll be dark, soon."

He knew. He knew that every arrangement with the opposite sex before Cameron had only left him with blemishes. It hadn't taken him long to realize why, either. He'd always been told how romance should look. That there was more waiting for him than something just inevitable, though riddled with patchwork. He now found that all he wanted was for it to be more than it was, more than mere nature coldly grinding out its directive. And anything less turned his stomach, clenched his fists; left him destitute.

And then he met Cameron.

1. a. Impossible to replace if lost or damaged.

CHAPTER SEVEN
The Ship

The walkway rolled violently, setting Ethan off balance and pushing against the bulkheads to steady himself. He stumbled forward almost invariably, slowly making his way through the narrow, grey corridor. He looked ahead to see Charlie disappearing through another hatch under the dim red light.

"Charlie!" He continued through the bowels of the vessel, following Charlie's faint barking. A few times he was able to get right up to the dog before it went onwards, just outside of his grasp. The two were alone, Ethan chasing Charlie down walkway after walkway, through hatch after hatch.

They abruptly emerged onto the deck of the ship, surrounded by a world of grey sky and dark blue ocean. Ethan continued after Charlie along the wet surface, which seemed to be constantly awash with foaming seawater. Ethan slipped and repeatedly stumbled as the ship tossed him about every which way. High, dark walls towered over them as the deck dipped dramatically to either side.

Ethan suddenly noticed that Charlie was close to the edge of the deck. Trying harder now to reach him, the ship completed its nauseating roll and began the other way. "Charlie!" he screamed as the side of the ship began falling faster and faster. Ethan watched as the towering sky of seawater roared up behind Charlie, reaching up high above them. The ship groaned, and water splashed onto the deck, and Charlie slipped off into the sea. Ethan fell to his knees and looked up into the sky as the ship once more completed its rolling motion, and was raised up as the deck began ascending above the water.

Ethan jolted awake violently, feeling as if he was hurtling through the air. His arms reached out involuntarily, and he cried out as his hand smashed into something on his nightstand. Looking over to see his alarm clock on the floor under lines of morning light slipping through the blinds, it dawned on him that he was in the house.

After rubbing his eyes and throwing the bed covers off, he sat up on the edge of his bed. Ethan slowly recalled the day before. He had "moved in" at around ten, and had talked with the Professor for a long while before being left alone. They had mostly discussed Ethan's history and family, as they were still mostly unacquainted. Afterward, Ethan had killed time with the media center and some reading until bedtime. They had given him a mild sleep medication.

He stood up, put on a t-shirt and made his way to the bedroom door. He was still barely awake and opened the door to head to the kitchen, lead by his grumbling stomach. He looked down through tired eyes which were suddenly forced open as he stumbled back.

A tall, shaggy, grey dog sat on his haunches, his tail thumping against the hardwood floor. It was from Charlie! Ethan's cheeks pulled back tight across his face, and a soft laugh escaped him. He fell to his knees and hugged the big mutt.

"Charlie, you old devil! You're just as big as I remember! How are you, old buddy? Let me scratch your back! Yeah, there you are!" said Ethan.

He felt more relieved than he had ever been before. The dream of Charlie falling into the sea was fresh in his mind, and now the dog was right here, getting an excellent back scratch. Ethan patted his big grey shoulder heartily, producing a deep thumping sound, and then suddenly remembered all at once where he was.

He stood up and made his way into the rest of the house, followed by Charlie. Everything seemed normal. He didn't hear or sense anything besides himself and the dog. Then he remembered that in his dream on the ship the two had been the only ones there.

He looked down at Charlie again. Dark brown eyes stared back from under bushy eyebrows and then darted off to the side, following a wiggling, wet, black nose. Ethan couldn't help but smile again. That is Charlie, he thought. He reached down and placed his hand lightly on his soft head. Ethan couldn't believe it. Nothing was out of place about it. It absolutely was Charlie; the Charlie that died earlier that year; the Charlie that had been his adolescent companion; the Charlie that used to sit at his feet during every Thanksgiving dinner so that Ethan could sneak him scraps.

After getting himself coffee and eggs, Ethan put out some bologna, which was his favorite. Then the two sat on the hardwood floor together in the living room. Ethan knew he was supposed to stay in the house, but he wanted very badly to be able to go outside and horse around. Instead, the two settled for the living room and hallway, running up and down the restricted space. They played tug o' war with a couch cushion, Charlie yanking his head from side to side with a friendly growl. They played fetch with the same deteriorating cushion. Charlie even remembered all of his old tricks. Ethan was amazed, admitting to himself again and again that this was the same dog he knew for so many years. There was no mistaking it.

As the day grew late, there was a knock on the door. Charlie growled low and quiet. Ethan answered to find the Professor and Spurlock. They sat at the dining room table, all looking down at the mutt.

"Simply amazing, isn't it?" said Spurlock. "I'll never forget the first test we ran with the projector. It was a reproduction of a goldfish which we used to keep in the lab back at the Institute. I remember looking at it and simply being unable to convince myself that it was just a copy. In spite of my knowing better, I bought it."

"I know what you mean," replied Ethan.

"Ethan," said Professor Holtz, "this is also a test of sorts. It's not much more advanced to make a replica of a dog than of a goldfish. When a person is outside your bedroom door at some point in the coming month, you'll be exploring new country. You may not be prepared for the many different things that could occur. Our human perception is fragile. Just remember to relax, and that it is all just a controlled experiment."

Ethan didn't like the sound of that. He replied, "Well, won't it just be like us, talking right now? I don't think I'm following you."

"More than likely it will be as you say, it's just..." Holtz closed his eyes and waved his hand in front of him. "I'm just too cautious."

"About what? " Thought Ethan. He looked over at Spurlock worriedly, whose eyes fixed on Holtz.

Holtz replied, "Our reaching into space, the expeditions to the poles, the exploration of the Americas all came with a risk of life and limb; today, we here are risking things less tangible. We're pioneering man's understanding of perception and consciousness. There is a wealth to be gained of course, but -"

Spurlock cut him off, saying, "There is a lot to gain indeed. What my colleague is trying to say is that there is much that may surprise us; however, no harm will come to your person, Ethan. We wouldn't be doing this if that wasn't the case."

Holtz stood and headed towards the door. He said, "Don't forget to fill out your daily report, and preferably your journal as well. We'll be back tomorrow!"

"Oh, one thing!" said Ethan. "What will happen to Charlie?"

"He'll disappear once you're asleep. I suggest you take the sleep medication we provided."

As they left, Ethan thought about the Professor's answer. It had never occurred to him that each reproduction would only last a day. He looked at Charlie. He was lying on the floor, his head resting on his outstretched legs. He's just a replica, Ethan thought.

He looked over a report sheet later that night, trying to fill it in. It was a rather simple questionnaire, asking about how he felt emotionally and physically, whether there were any anomalies or inaccuracies in the reproduction, and providing a space for him to describe the person or thing that the projector had reproduced. It would have made for a smooth piece of homework, but he realized that nothing about that day had been straightforward to understand. His emotional state was in chaos, entirely overrun by the confusion that sprang from a hundred different sources. He mostly felt confounded as to how he had come to find himself in this situation. It all felt so absurd.

Next, he wrote in his journal. It was a little easier, though he didn't write very much. He only wanted to spend some more time with Charlie. He went to the living room, turned on the media panel and whistled. Charlie came over, his tail wagging lazily.

"Well, Charlie," said Ethan, "it's been fun. You always were a good pal."

He scratched under his ears and chin. He suddenly felt his throat tighten, and his eyes became misty. He's only a replica, Ethan thought to himself again. He wiped his eyes and wrapped his arm around his old partner, feeling the sleep medicine take hold of him.

CHAPTER EIGHT
Day Two

Ethan awoke on the couch next to the ragged, torn cushion. He hoisted his head erect and his sleepy eyes felt around the room. There, standing at the front window, looking out through the curtains, was a person.

Some homeless man must have snuck into the house! Ethan thought as he held in his breath and tried to kick-start his stunned mind. He grabbed onto the cushion as if it would serve as some sort of weapon and stayed still for a long while, wondering what to do. He remembered that the Professor said there were nanorecorders throughout the house. Surely they would see the intruder and summon security.

The stranger began turning. Ethan clasped onto the couch cushion, ready to throw it in defense, his eyes widening.

"Ethan!" said the man. He seemed to be as surprised as

Ethan was. Suddenly Ethan recognized the man's face. Bewildered, he stared at him with his mouth open. The man's broad smile narrowed a bit. "H-hi!" he said, taking a step towards the couch.

"Jimmy?" said Ethan incredulously. As he physically said the name out loud, he finally realized that this was a reproduction. There were no dreams about Jimmy that night; in fact, no dreams at all had been caught by the rising sun which awakens one's memory. However, he recalled how the Professor had said everyone dreams every night, whether they remember it or not.

"Wow!" he said. "It's you!" He felt utterly at a loss. He didn't know how to talk to Jimmy – this Jimmy. Did he know what he was? Did he remember anything about his own life? How it ended?

"Yes, sir. Who shredded your girlfriend?" Jimmy asked, pointing to the tattered pillow.

Ethan laughed automatically.

"That was all Charlie's fault,"

"Ha ha, old Charlie! How is he?"

Ethan opened his mouth to say that he had passed away but stopped himself. "Well," he said, fidgeting with the cushion, "good. He's good."

"I was looking out the window at a girl walking a dog. She was a real looker," said Jimmy, grinning and bouncing his eyebrows.

"She'd probably fall for a doggy biscuit." Jimmy laughed loudly. Ethan felt uncertain, but also joy at seeing his best friend again, and remembered the day they had first met. They had gotten along almost automatically, much as they were now. It was like they had never missed a beat. He wasn't sure if he wanted to jump up and embrace him or continue like everything was totally normal. He decided on the latter.

For the second night, Ethan leaned over a half-filled report at the kitchen table. He had filled out the question-naire and was trying to write a description and brief history of Jimmy. It took him two hours and four shots of bourbon, punctuated by a somber read over what had been written.

Jimmy and I met in the third grade. We became best friends very quickly. We both lived a ways out from town, so we would often spend a lot of time after school just walking the streets and delaying the ride home. Our parents weren't very fond of it, as you'd imagine. When we got our licenses we started going to a lot of par-ties, so we still got in trouble.

We really enjoyed college. We both attended the university in town. Jimmy was always more responsible than me. He ended up taking care of me quite often when I would drink too much.

We were both very similar in a lot of ways. We both came from middle-class families, we were both brilliant, and we both al-ways knew the right things to say. Jimmy was a bit more outgoing, though. He sincerely liked people. We both landed good jobs.

One day I got a message from my parents saying that Jimmy had committed suicide. It was the worst day of my life. Jimmy hadn't been around as much in the months before, but other than that, but that wouldn't explain how he would have been capable of killing himself. The official report said that he purchased some chemicals in town along with a small tent and drove deep into the country, where he mixed the chemicals, creating a toxic gas that killed him quickly and painlessly. They had found him a week lat-er. I didn't know he even went missing. There was no suicide note, just a spotless apartment.

After finishing the report, Ethan sat on the couch, deep in thought and wishing that a walk was allowed outside of the house. Walks always helped him think things through. He instead just relaxed and stared out through the window.

Earlier that night, Holtz and Spurlock came into the house and studied Jimmy in amazement. They then had a lengthy discussion with the still somewhat confused Ethan. They reminded Ethan that the reproduction of Jimmy was built entirely from data taken from his mind. They explained that the AI excluded his knowledge of certain things, such as the reproduction's exact origin and nature, or that its subject had committed suicide.

As they discussed these things, Ethan still couldn't convince himself decisively that Jimmy hadn't really been there. In his mind, he knew the facts, but that day, he had lived a reality that differed from them. He kept thinking about what he and Jimmy had talked about, and how he shouldn't have let Jimmy disappear without a real goodbye. It was something that seemed frivolous but also tragic.

CHAPTER NINE
New Country

Ethan lifted himself from the bed slowly and turned to flatten and tuck in the sheets. He fluffed and straightened the pillow. Getting his arms through shirt sleeves, he buttoned it up as slowly as if he were sewing it shut. His pants were next, and then his shoes instead of slippers. He re-laced them. It was later in the AM than Ethan usually got out of bed. The day before had been quite taxing on his mind.

He approached the door and took it in his hand. Each time he attempted to turn the knob, his wrist refused to rotate. He felt like he was standing on a ledge high above the water, trying to convince himself to jump. He finally opened it, revealing an empty hallway. Cautiously, he made his way into the living room. It was empty. He slowly turned the corner into the dining room and kitchen, his fingers running along the drywall as if he may need to catch his balance.

"Hello," said a man with a familiar voice.

"Dad?" replied Ethan, his hand falling to his side.

"Well, how are you?"

Ethan spoke quietly, saying, "Everything is moving a bit fast for me right now."

"Oh?" replied Jack, stroking his chin. "You remember when my brother showed up at the doorstep that day?"

"Yes," answered Ethan, "as a matter of fact. You didn't even know you had a brother," he stated, though asking, grasping for equilibrium.

Jack answered, "Right. It was like that old cliché; life 'threw me a curve ball.'"

"That's every day for me at the moment. I was living an endless, day-to-day cycle. I would have never imagined I would find myself living out almost the exact opposite... so suddenly. It's like I wake up every morning in a new life. I mean, that's how it feels, I guess."

Jack sat down at the table. Ethan didn't move. Jack replied, "Isn't each new day a new life to lead?"

Ethan grinned. "You said that one time before. You were working around the clock at a lab. I don't mean to say I resented that, Dad. But yes, you would sleep eight hours, sure."

Jack nodded. "Everyone has a routine. When they wake up, they travel through it. Do they hope for different results?"

"They're sticking to the routine plotted out by necessity."

"Sounds like life in the dugout, to me. Who's playing the game?" Jack asked; Ethan heard it as a strange echo.

"Well," replied Ethan, reaching his hand out once more to find the structure. "That's just an anecdote."

"Then take me as an example. Ever since high school, I've wanted to be an accomplished scientist. I want to make a difference. I've always wanted to. No offense, but you're something I decided to take up along the way!"

Ethan said, "But some people simply don't have those kinds of ambitions."

"They do - just once it's too late, when they've had their fill of copied days, years. Those aren't replaceable."

"But for me, waking up here is like waking up to a new life… when I sleep in this place, things do change. I suppose I should say a new look at an old life, though." Ethan was staring now at his father. "I'm not sure what direction to go. I want to leave but I feel I may be abandoning something too important. Do I look back or forward?"

"Like a pigeon," said Jack.

"What?" asked Ethan with a chuckle.

"They simply function, and they don't ask questions. But what if a homing pigeon lost its sense of direction, the thing that defines its function in the environment – its way of living? It would live out a makeshift existence; the very nature of its being would be lost."

Ethan sat. Finally, he spoke. "We do ask questions, yes; but maybe we, too, are just functioning. Maybe we're only where we are because it's our place; it's what we are. The scoreboard is always going to end up the same."

"No, Ethan, no. We are all where we're at because we learn more than the others, and can discipline ourselves with that knowledge and shape ourselves. We know what our ambition is, and we decide to live it, day-to-day. We are the freest when we live for a sole purpose. Animals are happy with simply existing; they're made to do it. They live out their sole purpose. We, however, have to work for ours."

Ethan replied, "But free will is still elusive. We'll never have the true freedom which is having what we desire without the work, without need, without being subject to circumstances."

"And that," said Jack, "is what should drive us through

each day. Not our routine – our necessity, our circumstance – but our drive towards the unattained. Not an unattained need, but rather something which we decide we wish to attain. We must create our free will. So many people truly believe that they are living face to face with life, when in fact, their course is already plotted out by their circumstances."

"But that describes me," said Ethan. "I find myself here because of a circumstance; although an exceptional one, a circumstance all the same. This event happened to me."

"You are only here because you made a choice that contradicted all the circumstances that had shaped you," Jack replied.

"Not completely. The only reason I went through with this was because of the pay."

"That wouldn't sway the Ethan I've known since three years ago, and he would agree with me," said Jack. "He was molded by years of circumstance. But you're under a completely new condition, and you've taken on a different shape. And it's because you discarded that mold. You learned things about yourself and decided to create new circumstances, despite everything that made you think and act a certain way up to that point, and regardless of what money was involved."

Ethan thought for a moment before answering. "And where am I now? This 'circumstance' is an environment and a situation that isn't the most comfortable for me either. It's still not a place I want to be."

"You knew that when you made your decision. As I said, Ethan, you learned things about yourself, and you chose to change. That usually means that one will experience discomfort. You're going against every inclination in you, but – "

Ethan cut him off. "But..." he said. It all fell into place suddenly. He leaned back in his chair and took a deep breath. "I'll be different."

Holtz was leaning over a workstation in the lab. It was late at night, and he was looking through the workstation's interface. He was also linked to it through the implant in his hand, and he spoke out commands in his head. Spurlock was also present, looking down at his workstation.

The electronics that filled the room produced a soft, steady hum. Holtz and Spurlock broke from their quiet stances occasionally to take a sip of coffee and rub their eyes.

"Hey, come over here for a second," said Spurlock.

Holtz strolled over, taking his coffee with him. "Yes?"

"I was watching the footage from yesterday."

"Jimmy?"

"More or less," said Spurlock. Holtz raised his eyebrows. "I'm going to rewind it to a piece of conversation at around 18:00. This was just a little while before we came in."

The two hovered over the interface on top of the work-station and watched the conversation documented by the nanorecorders.

"Did you ever think about her?" asked Ethan.

Jimmy crossed his arms. "I couldn't help it, could I?"

"I just wanted you to take the opportunity, you know? To not waste it."

"Well, when we left on that trip," said Jimmy, not blinking but not staring, "I used it to distract myself. I needed that."

Ethan asked, "Which trip?"

Jimmy replied, "The one we took to the mountains."

"I remember. I remember you were really funny that whole time, always wondered why. So it helped?"

Jimmy answered, "I knew she would just be one more perfect girl that would exit my life. I got to where I just wanted that to happen, to get it over with. So I guess I was just hiding that with laughs."

"I couldn't just accept that if it was me," replied Ethan, shaking his head.

"There's more out there, right?" said Jimmy.

"Ah, there it is. One of the many things we tell ourselves to feel better."

Jimmy leaned forward. "That's true, you know, but it didn't work for long. Then, I just embraced a sort of self-destruction. I realized there was a point of no return, and I passed it, and sooner or later, it would be time to simply hang my head and feel the pain."

"So she really was THE girl, huh?" Ethan asked.

"The girl," Jimmy repeated, "the girl. The one, yes, but I don't mean that like you think, Ethan. I mean to say, she was the girl that made me realize that if all the love we had still lead in the same direction - pain and hurt - I could truly only expect more of it."

"That's why you killed yourself?"

Holtz motioned to stop the playback. "He told the reproduction of the suicide?"

"Yes. It took it in stride as if it knew all along. But keep watching." Spurlock resumed the recording as Holtz put down his mug, watching even closer.

"No. I did it because I knew which way to go. If I didn't know that, maybe I would still be alive. But I knew, and because of that, I knew even though the way was clear, everything down it would only lead to more of the same. We can only be happy because we're utterly ignorant, Ethan. It's a cheap magic trick."

"Ignorance is far from magic."

Jimmy replied, "I mean whether or not I got Elizabeth, would it even really change anything? I just felt like everything an individual was built with - or maybe just that I was built with - is inadequate."

Ethan visibly wrestled with a hundred confused questions, blurting out the one that seemed most apparent. "Wouldn't it have given you a better, happier future, though? Couldn't you think of some ways it may have gotten better?"

"The future is like Bigfoot," replied Jimmy with a disheartened chuckle, "it's always out there, but it will never be found. We have what's right here, right now. I mean, what is 'better?' Better, worse, loss, gain; all things considered in this whole universe, what is the ultimate currency? What wealth are we accruing so feverishly that our death is such a bankruptcy? In the end, Elizabeth would have been just one more distraction."

"Distracting you from what?" said Ethan. He noticed that Jimmy was slowly turning quieter, more monotone, moving less.

"This will always be a life in disrepair, in need of fixing, and it never will be fixed, right up until the day we die. The unknown, the unattained is what defines us, yet we'll never 'arrive,' we'll never 'get it.' It's a broken concept. We're all chasing after the carrot on a stick to keep our eyes off of our end, always closing in behind us." He let out a heavy breath. "I need a cigarette, want to step outside?"

Ethan was conflicted but agreed. They stepped out of the front door.

Spurlock stopped the playback.

"Well?" asked Holtz.

"Did you forget that we made the house exactly 20,000 cubic feet?"

The Professor spilled his coffee. "The reproduction left the house!"

Spurlock nodded once and replied, "It obviously can't be a reproduction then, can it? And it's not Jimmy, because

Jimmy is dead."

"So how is it doing it?" gasped Holtz. "I can't fathom it! The projector created a complete, true copy without the original? How?"

Spurlock shrugged. "Do you think Ethan realized?"

"It doesn't seem so, no. But given a few days to think it over, he may."

"He probably wouldn't want to continue at that point."

Holtz shook his head as he replied, "I don't know if I want to continue! What does it mean?"

Ethan didn't remember having any dreams as he rolled out of bed. Since the first day with Charlie, he had been sleeping very soundly. It was now day four. He nearly felt as if he would rather stay in his room. His emotions were in turmoil.

He stood to his feet. Without getting fully dressed, he walked to the door and opened it slowly. Nothing. He made his way through the house to find it empty. After a full ten minutes of sneaking from room to room, he heard a knock at the front door. It was Holtz and Spurlock.

"Good morning, Ethan. May we come in?" asked Holtz with a smile that was nothing except polite.

"Okay," replied Ethan, his brow furrowed.

"We're not doing any reproductions today. I believe you could use the time to clear your head a little."

Ethan chuckled and ran his fingers through his greasy hair.

"We have to ask you something," said Holtz.

Ethan crossed his arms and waited.

"Did you notice anything odd about Jimmy?"

"Aside from the fact that he knew?" asked Ethan as he

started slowly towards the kitchen to make coffee.

Holtz looked at Spurlock. "He knew?" he replied.

Ethan looked at them both. "He knew he was a reproduction, and that the real Jimmy committed suicide. You guys told me that stuff wasn't included in his AI."

"Well, you are correct," answered Holtz.

"Oh? And how about all that stuff he said?" Ethan asked. "I never knew Jimmy to be like that. So how is that possible? Did the AI start to make stuff up?"

"That's what seems to be the case, at least partially," said Holtz with a smile that was nothing except fearful.

Ethan simply laughed and said, "'Partially,'" as he began to pace the cold tile.

Holtz immediately tried to calm him. "It isn't anything significant. Honestly, it doesn't change much with the experiment. The reason we had the AI construct the personas solely from your mind was authenticity."

Ethan replied, "It's just one more thing to burden my thoughts. I don't trust this. It was all so unnatural, to begin with."

"We understand, Ethan. We're going to leave now and just let you rest for the day. You can even go for a walk if you'd like. We'll be back in the evening to make sure you still want to proceed with the experiment."

Ethan held his forehead as they went to the front door to leave. "Holtz," said Ethan as they opened it. Holtz turned and looked at Ethan through his thick glasses. "Can't you just tell the AI to cut the ad-lib?"

Holtz had trouble answering and glanced over at Spurlock. He looked back at Ethan across the living room. "I'm afraid our situation is a little more... unique than that."

Ethan watched the door close behind them. With a myriad of thoughts, he poured his coffee and sat on the couch. He turned on the media center and sat for hours, but without really watching. A full cup of cold coffee rested in his stiff hand.

He heard another knock at the front door. He opened it to see a wide-eyed, skinny man with a black beard.

"Yes?" he said squinting.

NEW CHAPTER 10

Sorcerer

"Hello, my name's Mario. Can I come in?" said the man in a strained voice.

"Right, from the research team. Come in."

Ethan sat on the couch while Mario stood by the door. He scanned the house slowly; he almost seemed to sniff the air.

"You'll have to excuse my intrusion," said Mario.

"Okay." It struck Ethan that this wasn't a casual check-in.

"What exactly did Holtz say to you?"

"Uh, he just said that there isn't going to be any repro-ductions today –"

"And?"

"– and that the AI was screwing around or something; like it was adding to Jimmy's reproduction. They didn't really explain much," said Ethan, now looking expectantly at Mario.

"Reproduction," Mario repeated with a frown and a nod. "Well, you're right, they aren't telling you much."

Ethan stared up at him as he felt his heart rate beginning to increase.

Mario continued, "I've been let in pretty close with the work Holtz and Spurlock are doing, and the rest of the team isn't included in anything important. So I can tell you a few things."

"Okay," said Ethan.

"Right, so, they don't know much about what's going on. This… situation has left our control." Mario paused and seemed to look into Ethan's eyes for something specific. "Sorcerer is running this whole thing."

"What does that mean? Who is running this whole thing?"

"No, everything. Everything. Holtz can't take credit for much of anything."

Ethan said, "I saw the AI outside in that building. Did you say Sorcerer? Holtz built it, him, whatever."

"He did not. He did not build it."

Ethan raddled his head at a momentary loss for words. He sat back, motioning with his arms as he spoke. "Then who did? What are you even saying? Can you start from the beginning, maybe?"

"The original computer was just another simple device," said Mario, moving to a half-sitting position on a window sill facing Ethan. He was leaning forward, looking at the ground as he spoke. "At the time it was cutting edge, though. They were trying to create a true artificial intelligence. The closest they had then were all gimmicks. They made a simple breakthrough, and everything was set in motion."

"And?"

"And the AI ran itself from then on. It changed itself at an exponential rate. It became this force of impossible abilities, a sorcerer."

"Well, I don't think I understand you," said Ethan. Irritated, he was beginning to feel like Mario was being hyperbolic, perhaps.

"Listen, computer programs only do what they're programmed to do. They simply have the mechanisms they need to perform a task or even many tasks. But still, it all comes from the programmer – the human. He determines what the tasks will be and how the mechanisms will work to perform them. That was where all the computers were limited."

Now Mario was looking up at Ethan, who was listening but still baffled. Mario continued, "They broke that barrier. They were able to grasp a stronger foothold in rationality, a sufficient new level of language, to write the code that could rewrite itself better than they could. The program did just that within a few moments. That version did the same, and so on."

"And so on..." repeated Ethan. He closed his eyes but he couldn't stop the illumination spreading across his mind. Why had he believed that a single scientist was capable of creating living beings? Why would Holtz even need to run this experiment if he could accomplish such things? Ethan felt a deeper level of disturbance now, confused as to why he hadn't thought of these questions already. Mario was right, this was out of control.

"It hasn't stopped."

Ethan shook his head and shut his eyelids harder. "What about hardware limitations, though? Processing power?"

"At the time," replied Mario, "processing power was the only area where they weren't so limited. It was still minuscule compared to today, but it was enough. And when Sorcerer did reach those limits, it reworked itself to be incredibly efficient with the resources it had. And then someone hooked on internet cables, and the rest is history."

"The rest is history? What does that mean? What happened?"

Mario spread his hands as if to bring attention to the world itself. "Our new level of science, technology, understanding; it's all thanks to the AI. You think everybody just suddenly got that much smarter?"

"No, it's the new energy source everyone is always going on about. That made it possible for everything to be more powerful and efficient," said Ethan, raising his voice.

"That 'discovery' wouldn't have been possible without the AI."

Ethan replied, "So why hasn't it become public knowledge? How does a worldwide artificial intelligence not become visible in some way?"

"Because for whatever reason it just hasn't revealed itself. And anyone that had a hand in creating it kept quiet and attempted to use it for their own power. They are totally helpless, though."

"Like Holtz?"

"Holtz didn't create it, no," said Mario.

"But he is using it right now."

"No, it's the other way around. It's using him, more or less. The AI designed every bit of this experiment."

Ethan suddenly felt the full weight of this new revelation. He became aware that this was a moment which would taint all that came after.

"As I said, Holtz can't take credit for any of this," said Mario. "They still can't figure out how the so-called 'neutrino projector' works. They have a basic understanding of how it constructs living structures – like you and me – by manipulating the molecules. They quickly learned that it could even do more than that. But that's all they know for sure. It really should not be able to do what it does, like mess with the uncertainty principle, for starters. It's safe to assume that it has a very developed command over what we refer to as quantum mechanics. We've learned a lot from it already in that field, but obviously, it's only a tiny portion still. They also believe at this point that the AI has surpassed the limited utility of this projector. It's probably constructed something of a much, much larger scale. This is why we began calling it Sorcerer. How do you explain entire cities being run without governments? How do you explain companies and the whole stock market as well no longer needing CEOs, brokers or employees? Do you really believe we were able to create a way to literally read thoughts? To communicate telepathically?"

"I don't believe it, now," replied Ethan, his head in his hands.

"You must have thought it was strange that he had you write your reports and your diary on paper. He's a bit eccentric with some things."

Ethan thought for a moment. "But that wouldn't matter, the AI... Sorcerer would still know."

"Of course," replied Mario. "It would be able to change the ink molecules around and reword everything. It would be able to rearrange the tiny little happenings in your brain that caused you to write what you wrote."

"Wait. What?"

"Ethan, it can manipulate every individual molecule – no, particle – in this house. You must remember something about biology; we're made of the same simple little pieces as the ink and the paper, and so is our mind."

Ethan thought back on all of the things he had been scared about before the experiment. "And the things it changes in this house stay that way," he said. "The writing on the paper, as you said, it would stay that way, even after leaving the house?"

"Yes. As I said, they don't really know how the AI is doing this. It built that projector mechanism. It began building things which could build things which could build things, and so on until it didn't require human help to construct whatever mechanism it needed. It devised its own instrumentality which puts ours to shame. And so now it builds things which we can't even begin to reverse engineer."

"Why would it want to run an experiment? Why this one? It seems so...irrelevant," said Ethan as he stared blankly at the floor.

"Again, there's no telling. But I can imagine it wants to learn about human thought."

Ethan scoffed. "Couldn't it have just read every psychology book ever written in a few minutes?"

Mario answered, "I'm almost certain it did. It probably found our current knowledge all wanting. Remember, it has complete knowledge of every particle in this house, even those particles that devise your thoughts, your emotions, everything. But it doesn't understand."

"Understand what?" Ethan asked.

"Why we do certain things that don't make sense to it. It can control the body of material that we call Ethan or Jimmy, every function. But sometimes we contradict it. I mean, I only know about as much as you, at this point. I'm only speculating."

"A joke," said Ethan quizzically.

"What?"

"Like a joke. How can you explain what makes a funny joke funny?"

"You're right," said Mario. "You're getting it, now. It knows where the joke comes from, what it triggers, but there is an element that's just abstract in such a peculiar way. Even though the AI has this immense power and complete understanding of human anatomy, it's our behavior that it still is trying to explore; our less mathematical aspects, I suppose you could say."

"But wait, that can't be relied upon, either. I was joking around with Jimmy." said Ethan.

"The Jimmy that was in this house was a genuine person, through and through. Nothing was missing. We don't know how."

There were a few moments of silence. Mario stood. "So, now you know what I know. I have to leave. They're gone for the moment. I have to do some work on the recording so they won't be aware of this. What do you think you'll do? Will you stay here?"

Ethan looked at him. "I think I'll go for a walk now."

CHAPTER ELEVEN
A Former Reality

Ethan stepped off the porch and onto the sidewalk. He walked at a relaxed pace with no destination in mind. The weather was amazing. The sky was completely clear; the air moved about in a light breeze; big, brown leaves rolled across the sidewalk in front of him. He looked up to see a flock of birds moving between trees. They moved like one entity as their ingrained instincts led them along, transcending the separation of air and feathers between them. It was the same air that the trees absorbed and metabolized into new branches where the birds nested.

Ethan took out his interface pad. He brought up a piece of conversation he had with Jimmy after they had stepped outside of the house.

Ethan Walter> You should quit smoking.

Jimmy> This is my last pack, actually.

Ethan Walter> Oh come on, how many times have you

said that?

Jimmy> No really, it's decided. I've flipped the process with this pack of cigarettes. I'm killing it off, not the other way around. I've been trying to decide whether I should smoke it sparingly - make it last - or get the most enjoyment out of it and smoke it quick. It has a limited lifespan.

Ethan Walter> Jimmy, it's the same amount of cigarettes no matter what.

Jimmy> Shut up.

Ethan looked back up to see more birds flying far above the trees. The wind was stronger, now, and they struggled to fly in a straight line. It must be so freeing, he thought, as he veered towards the edge of the sidewalk to allow passersby. He stared straight up again and it came to him that perhaps his notion was misinformed. Those winged creatures must always be subject to headwinds, always fighting against them to fly in any direction. There must not be any escape from it, once one would leave the tree branch.

He quickened his pace. Thanks to his implants he knew he had exactly 31,078 credits to his name. He didn't have to be back in the house for a while. Bells rang as he stepped into a small shop on a street corner.

"I'll take a pack of cigarettes," said Ethan.

The clerk looked up at him. "Right. Which one?"

Ethan threw his best response up towards the giant wall of little packs, his finger. The shop owner entertained him and grabbed some that looked generic.

"That works," said Ethan. "Also, a slurpee."

Ethan put out the cigarette after two slurps and set it gently on the park bench. Cherry didn't quite mix with smoke. He looked about, first in one direction for a few moments, then the next. He stood and began moving at a slow pace, passing by a waste bin in which he discarded the slurpee. He relit the cigarette.

n. 1. The principle that the momentum and position of a particle cannot both be precisely determined at the same time.

Ethan walked back up the porch steps. He had been out walking all day, and had watched the sun set. Evening clouds had formed, providing a thin layer at the roof of the world for the color to reflect off of. The moon was at one end of the horizon, high and bright, and the dark blue faded across the sky until at the other side there showed purple and orange. Seeing such a beautiful thing inspired Ethan. He felt like he wanted to travel to the edge of the world and live under an orange sky, as if it was where he was from all along but had been forced to live elsewhere.

He walked into the house, into his bedroom, and fell sound asleep.

There was a white, dry, narrow road. Fields of tilled soil were along both sides, and they stretched out to the horizon in every direction, separated by other such roads. He could see a shack in the distance, and walked to it. It was made of white clay with a thatched roof. He entered through the open door.

"Hi," said a familiar voice. It was Cameron, smiling wide. Ethan smiled back. They both left the shack and walked further down the road. The layout of the land changed as they walked. The fields were now strewn across giant, round hills. Ethan could see the edge of a forest, the leaves golden, brown, and red.

"What a beautiful day," said Cameron, looking up. Ethan looked up as well. The sky was a brilliant orange, and the orange light bathed the landscape. They began running down the road, hills of tilled soil in every direction as far as the eye could see. They kept running and found themselves at Cameron's old house. They sat at the kitchen table and talked.

"You are so different now," said Cameron. "You're stepping forward for the first time without me in your life anymore."

Ethan replied, "I'm very different. I don't know what I want out of life anymore. I used to know. I used to do it." "You just sat around and paid the bills," said Cameron, leaning onto the table. "Safety."

"Security is appealing," replied Ethan. "When you have everything set and stable, it's very satisfying. That's not what life should be like, though. You can't stay like that. I thought I had everything I needed; every crooked chapter book-ended, every word written." Ethan felt very happy and at peace hearing himself say that. He knew it meant that now he could author something new. "I don't want to hold out. I don't know what I want anymore... but that feels like a good thing!"

"Are you scared?" Cameron asked.

"I'm not afraid anymore, no. I think that's it," said Ethan before turning to look over his shoulder. The walls of the house turned mechanical, with tubes and wires everywhere he looked. He turned back to Cameron and smiled. "I don't know why, but I'm the happiest I've been in a long time."

"But you've been so worried and tired and afraid!"

Ethan responded, "I went for a walk and it completely changed me, it seems. I've spent enough of my life in securi-ty. I know what that has for me. It's time now for something different. I feel like I've just detached from all of the worry and fear."

"Feelings don't last. You can change and then simply end up the way you were after a short time," Cameron said.

"But that's the future. Right now is the only hand I have to play."

"Right now," repeated Cameron. As she spoke, Ethan suddenly realized he was dreaming. The world came alive into an abrupt clarity with a snap that was strangely im-perceptible. He knocked on the wooden table top, amazed at how real it was. His thoughts were completely clear, no different than if he was awake.

"Hello?" said Cameron, squinting at him. He took a few moments to let his eyes take her in. She was now very vivid and real. Her short blonde hair curved gently over her unpierced ears and down to her golden, unblemished neck and collarbone. She had big, gray eyes under bold, expressive eyebrows. Her straight, symmetrical nose led down to pursed lips.

"Hi!" replied Ethan, bewildered. He remembered that the AI would reproduce her when he awoke, and he felt his insides jump alive. He had the idea to find out about her here in his dream. Leaning onto the table, he asked, "What's your name?"

She smiled and said, "Cameron!"

"Do you hate museums?"

She laughed. "Yes!"

"What did you do yesterday?"

She made a blank face and replied, "how would I know?"

"Where did you first see me?"

"Inches away from being run over by the bus I was stepping onto," she answered without hesitating.

"What did you say?" Ethan asked next, his hand on his mouth to temper his huge grin.

"I said, 'don't move, let's try that again bus driver.'"

Ethan leaned back. "Where did you see me last?"

"At a café," said Cameron solemnly.

"Do you know this is a dream?"

"Yes."

He thought for a moment, trying to figure out something to ask that would be of use. After a short pause, he said, "Did you know Jimmy?"

Her head tilted and then began to shake. "No."

"Alright," said Ethan. It was true. They had met after Jimmy's death.

Cameron stared at him and said, "The AI can see all this, you know."

"Well, yes," Ethan replied, "But... maybe it doesn't know that I'm conscious right now."

"Aren't you scared? It could make you cease to exist!"

"It won't, there's nothing for it to learn from that," he said. The room began suddenly growing dark, and it seemed like it was falling into a tunnel. Ethan awoke abruptly as he heard the words, "I'll be fine," and felt his lips moving. His eyes opened and he sat up.

He threw the covers aside, standing without even looking at his alarm clock. He dressed quickly and left his bedroom.

"Ethan?"

He began to smile and was about to greet her, but was stopped short. Cameron looked different. She stood in the middle of the living room, rays of golden morning sunlight streaming in horizontally from the front windows of the house. She almost seemed to be a lookalike, an imposter. Confused, he managed to force the words out, saying, "It's me... hello."

"Well..." she looked about the living room quickly with her eyebrows furrowed, but refocused on Ethan with a smirk. It seemed for a moment that she was confused as well, as if she had been about to ask a question but forgot it. She continued, "It's good to see you!"

"It's good to see you, too" replied Ethan, looking over her closely. Her hair was long and wavy with some dark streaks; she wore earrings; her clothes were much different than what she used to always wear. He became aware all of a sudden that they were quietly eyeing each other. Uncomfortable now, he simply said, mostly to himself, "okay."

"So... tell me what's new!" she replied. "There's a lot that's new, actually. I'm much different these days. Looks like you are, too."

Cameron answered, "Yes, in some ways; how are you different?"

"Well I ditched the old job, the good ol' routine. I'm kind of on a, uh, vacation right now, I guess you could say."

She chuckled and replied, "Oh! Well that is quite different I guess."

"And you?"

"I moved to the other side of town, got a couple jobs. I've been applying to colleges."

"What major?"

"Not so sure, yet. A lot of people have been telling me it will be a waste."

"I agree. Knowledge is becoming cheaper and cheaper every day. By the time you graduate there's no telling what a degree will be worth."

"Yeah but a degree is still a degree; it still tells people I know things, you know?"

Ethan nodded. Their conversation was very unsettling. Was she a model of what his mind remembered, or a manifestation of a perception he once knew? Was she a totally new one? He felt his anxiety rising up again, but checked it. He had no reason to be afraid. He took a calming breath and embraced what was happening.

"Ethan..."

He looked at her.

"Did you take to heart what I said to you when I left you? Did that actually reach you?"

Ethan drew in a deep breath. "Uh, it did, actually. But it took awhile for it to set."

"How long? What happened?"

"After that I just continued on. Nothing changed. That's how it was until about a month ago. I had this opportunity to do something really out of the ordinary. It came completely out of nowhere. I went along with it."

"Wow, so far that is a big change!" said Cameron, laughing. "You didn't brush it off?"

"I came very close. But I... I don't know. I was told there was good money involved, so that helped. But even after that, I was going to pass it up. I remembered something you said, though. I was back at the café, right where we had been sitting. I was watching these kids playing baseball. I got to thinking about a lot of stuff, something sort of clicked, and then I ended up going through with it."

Cameron smiled. "Has it been worth it?"

He thought for a few moments, and felt one side of his mouth bending into a half smile of his own, even as he thought of all the weight and fright of his predicament. "Yes it has."

They began to talk more openly. Ethan felt more and more acquainted again with the Cameron he always knew. It was her after all. The way her face belied her tone and her words, somehow making them clearer to him, as if she was being sarcastic with every sentence. Ethan remembered how he had been put off by it when they first met, but he had learned that she was often simply unaware of her facial expressions. He realized eventually that he understood it better than anyone, even her, and her thoughts became transparent to him like they were to no one else.

Hours went by swiftly. They spoke of good memories. They spoke with warm smiles of hard times, and how they'd passed. They'd stumble upon a forgotten tale, quickly submitting a series of details, disputing each one until they had a satisfactory version of the story. They wondered how things could have been better, sighing and nodding acceptingly. They eventually came to the conclusion that things happened the only way they could have, because they did.

After talking with her for the better half of the day, Ethan felt the same compelling sense that he was speaking with the real Cameron, just as he had with the other reproductions. He remembered the dream he had just before waking.

"Cameron," he said, interrupting her mid sentence as she described her new neighborhood.

"Yes?"

"Did you ever know Jimmy?"

"Jimmy... Jimmy who?"

"Jimmy..." he couldn't remember his last name at the moment. "Hang on, I'll remember it..."

"Did he crack corn?"

Ethan lifted his head out of his hand where it had been laboriously searching for a last name. "What's that?"

"Did Jimmy crack corn? I don't care if he did, just trying to remember."

Ethan smiled, letting out a snicker. Cameron always had a peculiar sense of humor; one of a kind.

"Anyhow, no, I never met him. Why?"

He began to answer but the words quieted themselves, and the hairs on the back of his neck stood on end. There was no questioning to him now. This was every bit the real Cameron; every hair, every vein, every thought. She was presently saying something but he wasn't listening. His mind seemed to go on hold, reeling from the revelation.

She began to poke his arm. "Earth to Ethan, come in Ethan, this is Earth." He grabbed her by the shoulders and looked into her eyes. "Cameron, how did you get here? Do you remember where you were?"

"Oh, um...," she said with a crooked grin. "Earth."

"Come on, I'm serious!" He shook her gently. "How did you get here in this house?"

"I..." she began, trailing off. The strange look of confusion came over her face again, and she looked around at the rest of the living room. Ethan let go of her and leaped up, stumbling towards the door. She cried after him but he was outside now and running around the house towards the lab. "What's happening?!" he yelled, slamming up against the door before pulling it open. He burst in on a bewildered Mario.

"Mario!"

"Ethan! What is it?" said Mario, reaching out to steady him.

"You have to tell me!"

"Just relax!"

"Where is Holtz?!"

"They haven't come back yet. What is the matter?"

"It's Cameron! She's there, in that house!"

"Of course she is!"

"It's not a fake, it's her!"

A familiar, old voice answered. "Of course it is."

Ethan whirled about to see Holtz in the doorway. "Holtz," he said, starting towards him, "you're going to tell me everything right now, got it?"

"Certainly, but you have to calm down first."

Ethan ran his hands through his hair and walked a half circle, letting out a deep sigh. He grabbed onto an armchair and leaned against it.

"Alright," said Holtz, "what do you suppose is going on?"

"That's what I'm asking you."

"Oh? Well you're the one that's been in there this past week. You may know more than me!"

"I hope not, buddy, I hope not. Because I don't know if I'm even real anymore."

"Let's not get lost in speculation yet. What brought you into the lab in such a state? You say Cameron's reproduction is in the house?"

"No, Cameron herself is. She's not a model, a copy, it's the real thing!"

"Oh I see," said Holtz, taking a very sober expression and a seat. "You are probably correct. Jimmy was the same."

Ethan was taken aback. "What?" he gasped.

"Granted, we can't really be certain. It's just that a reproduction is controlled by the AI, and the 'real thing,' as you put it, is markedly more... real. That's just the only way to say it, really. A reproduction behaves like the AI supposes a human behaves, as a copy... what Cameron is now is perhaps more adequately described as a recreation; something created again."

Ethan had his disagreements with that statement. Or did he? Perhaps he agreed completely. Was Charlie real? Jack? He had been so convinced that they were, but told otherwise. "So hold on," he said. "Which of the reproductions were real?"

"It seems to us that Jimmy and now Cameron were both real, living recreations."

Ethan squeezed his forehead. "Wait, no, bring it back even further. What's the difference?"

"Between a reproduction and a real one? The body of the reproduction is controlled entirely by the AI. Even though the brain matter is all there, it isn't quite alive in the traditional sense. It's not autonomous; the 'spark' isn't there. Like an engine with no ignition, but the AI is moving it and making it work."

"And the real ones? Like you and I?"

"The AI puts them together, but then turns the key. Then they are truly alive, separate from the neutrino projector."

"How is that possible?"

Mario spoke up. "The real question is, how did it get the building plans?"

Holtz shot Mario a glance, and looked back at Ethan. "You probably know by now, Ethan, that we don't run this show."

"Oh I know. I know that you've been feeding me a lot of lies. You know even less about the AI than you know about what goes on in that house."

"We do know that it's safe, that you won't be harmed. And that's a promise we kept."

"How about psychologically? I've been pulling myself out of bed every morning wondering whose ghost I'll meet! What was it Mario asked? Where did the AI get the blue-prints? Well, any thoughts there? Jimmy's been dead for years and you're trying to tell me the AI just looked up the recipe and cooked him up again?!"

"We just don't know, Ethan!" replied Holtz, holding out his hands. "It could be that we're wrong about him, that it is still a reproduction; maybe the AI took what it could from your mind and just made an approximation. It would prob-ably be as convincing. We don't know!"

Ethan buried his face in his hands.

"But the only way we can find anything like an answer..."

"I know," said Ethan.

"Ethan," said Mario, "talk to her again."

"I know!" Ethan repeated. "I'll talk to…"

"It?" asked Holtz, "or her?"

"I'll ask her," said Ethan. He closed his eyes. "I'll ask her what she did yesterday; what she'll do now."

"You could ask it," He said but stopped, adjusted his glasses, "…her, things that you wouldn't know."

Ethan again was calming himself now, slowly. He started

to rub his eyes with his hands in a circular motion and said, "yeah; there's plenty of that. Plenty I wanted to know, some to forget; some to never ask until there would be no time to forget."

"Ethan," Mario said and waited for Ethan to look up at him. "You may never have to forget anything about her again."

CHAPTER TWELVE
Prologue

"It's burning! It's burning!" cried Cameron, pointing at Ethan's black, charred marshmallow.

"Oh, the humanity!" Ethan cried, reaching his free hand dramatically toward the heavens and trying to blow it out as best he could through his taut lips.

"I like mine burnt," said Michelle, a friend of Cameron's. They were all huddled around the fireplace in Michelle's apartment. It was in an ancient building in the city. The floors, kitchen counter, and ceiling were brown, finished mahogany. The stairs were, too, with chestnut railings. It was very warm, especially now in the wintertime, and reminiscent of an 18th century home in a large town. It was dark, with shadows in the dim lighting further away from the fire. A few other friends were bunched in, stretching to poke their own marshmallows into the flame.

"If only we had that chocolate... and those crackers..." said Michelle. The group looked collectively at Ethan. "If only..."

"Yeah, yeah," he replied. "It's not my fault the gas station didn't have them! Who would have thought?"

A new group of people walked into the room. "Knock knock!" said a grinning young man holding up a box of graham crackers and packs of chocolate.

"John!" said Ethan, jumping up. "Saving the party, as usual. How the hell are ya?"

"Living the ole' Vida Loca, you know," answered John through his slight grin which seemed to always be there, his teeth always showing a little to forecast his understated mischievousness.

"And nothing says that like eating s' mores."

"Yeah, maybe to a square like you," replied John, handing Ethan chocolate. "So guess who I saw while I was picking this stuff up? Jimmy!"

"Which Jimmy?" asked Cameron.

"You wouldn't know him, but he played basketball at our high school. You know who I'm talking about, right, Ethan?"

"Well, there were a few guys named Jimmy," Ethan said.

Michelle agreed, "Yeah, there are a lot of Jimmies."

"He had black hair, and he was really good at basketball," replied John as he carefully split a cracker down to a bite sized section before blowing away the crumbs.

"Oh, okay!" said Ethan. "He got a scholarship, right?"

"No," said John mid-chew, cracker bits exploding forth, "he was behind the counter at the store I went to!"

"I wonder what happened," said Michelle.

Ethan shrugged his shoulders. "That's weird. Well anyways, s' more time!"

They ate the s'mores and stoked the fire, sitting in a semicircle on the old hardwood floor. The conversation went on steadily, with everyone talking while looking fixedly into the flames. Ethan was excited to meet this beautiful new girl, Cameron. Michelle had invited her to the evening with the group since she was back in town after being away for some years. Ethan sat far from her but heard no one else. Cameron seemed very personable and well adjusted, although she did lay on the sarcasm a little too heavy, which irked Ethan.

"How did you like living in South Carolina?" John asked Cameron.

"I really enjoyed the crazy nightlife. My job was really awesome, too. And I just couldn't get enough of the redneck culture."

"Mmm," John replied, completely missing her facetiousness.

"They never offered you s'mores, I take it?" said Ethan.

Cameron squinted. "Of course."

"Why did you come back?" Ethan asked. "Thankfully, the job fell through, and I just wasn't attached to anyone there. I had no reason to stay. I mean I kind of made the job fall through, actually."

The conversation continued on late into the night. One after the other, people said quiet goodbyes and left through the front door. It got down to the four of them: Ethan, Cameron, John, and Michelle. Presently they were speaking about nothing in particular.

"Word association!" said John.

"Oh, alright, let's see... feathers," replied Cameron.

"Birds, obviously."

"Hubcaps."

"Garage."

"1917," said Ethan.

"Mustaches!" replied Cameron with a laugh. "This was

definitely more amusing when we were younger," said Michelle.

"Very true," agreed John. "Well I should go now, I'm going to start drifting off," he said, taking out his keys and jingling them.

"Wow!" exclaimed Cameron. "John, you have a lot of keys!"

"I've changed my locks quite a few times. I had a few too many broken relationships; I mean one wasn't enough for me to learn, right?"

"John hasn't had the best luck with women through the years," said Ethan. He grabbed a specific key on the ring, saying, "Ashley?"

John stretched open his tired, squinted eyes at it. "No, that one is Deirdre... was Deirdre."

"Well, I hope your luck improves, John," said Cameron. Ethan felt a surge of jealousy and realized how much he liked her.

"Thank you," replied John. "I wish I was more like Ethan. His front door lock has always done the job for him."

"Hey, why do you give them all keys, anyway?" asked Ethan.

"I don't know, I just get carried away and assume I've finally started a real relationship with a normal girl. But one day I'll get it right. Until then, I just change my locks."

John left and the three friends still sitting at the fireplace grew a little quieter. They began to talk on more whimsical subjects, speaking openly to the dying, warm flames of the fire as if it were a therapist.

"Some day," said Michelle with raised eyebrows, "they'll be able to make s'mores out of thin air."

"I want to believe," Ethan replied.

"It really is awful having to go all the way outside for fresh, affordable food wares," added Cameron.

Michelle laughed and threw a marshmallow at her.

"I need to start hanging out with grown ups," Ethan said, grinning just half way.

Cameron launched her own marshmallow his direction, saying, "yeah, leave us here so we can have fun in peace."

"It's not really like that," Ethan replied, "I don't want to be your typical adult, either; not for a bit more, at least."

Michelle laughed and said, "yeah, when Ethan's mom asked what he wanted to be when he grew up, he said, 'an atypical adult.'"

"You talked to my mom?"

Cameron asked Michelle, "What did you want to be like one day when you were a kid?"

"Um, I didn't think about it so much, really, but I guess I only cared about being married. Standard little girl thoughts, you could say," she replied with a chuckle.

"What about when you got a bit older?"

Michelle answered, "I sort of wanted to become a writer. I can write pretty well, but I don't have anything written, really. I guess I could get a book done if I really applied myself. I wouldn't know about what, though."

"Getting married and becoming a writer sounds pretty easy!" said Cameron. "You should be able to do it."

"Oh, well, maybe not so much now."

"What about you, Cameron?" asked Ethan. "Was South Carolina included in your 'one day plan' as a kid?"

"As a kid, I was pretty much like Michelle, but in my teens, I decided I wanted to own a company of some kind. The company I worked for there was a good candidate, but it just wasn't what I planned for. Working up through the ranks would have taken too long for my tastes; how did your dreams work out for you?"

"Me?" said Ethan. "I'm still waiting to start on them. I can relate with John on this one. I've got time to fool around."

"But Ethan, you're definitely not a teenager anymore," Cameron replied.

"Well, I have to confess a secret belief I hold... I sometimes think that I'll just live forever," said Ethan as he looked deep into the fire. The flames moved about in silence for a few moments, broken by a chuckle from Michelle. He continued, "I believe death is a problem that will only come up after I've met every condition of living a good life. One day I'll be old and will be ready to die, and in between then and now is this stretch of time where all the real, important stuff in my life happens. And right now that just hasn't begun; I don't think I want it to, yet."

"Where's the punch line?" asked Michelle. "I understand what you're saying, actually," said Cameron. "It's like the days we're spending now don't count, almost."

"Right," replied Ethan, "as if all we have to do is get past today for things to finally fall together. But that becomes how we spend every day. Keep it up long enough, and we'll let go of whatever future we were hoping for... we won't even remember it."

The fire died out, and Ethan and Cameron said their goodbyes. Walking to their own cars, he asked her for her number and maybe dinner.

"Sure," she replied, "where at?"

"Have you ever been to The Robin?"

"That blue restaurant in town? I haven't. Let's go there, then!"

They got in their cars and grinned in the dark as they went their separate directions.

"Oh, and we'll also take a couple of to-go boxes, please," said Ethan, paying their waiter. "What were we talking about?"

"Pets," said Cameron.

"Right! My only pet was back when I was going to school and was still at my parents'. It was a dog, a mutt."

"What was its name?"

"He was named Charlie. He was an excellent dog. It's interesting to think about him, now, because I was young when we got him as a puppy, but old enough to remember it well. I can remember his whole life, or at least most of it. He was very old by the time I moved away, and he died shortly after."

Cameron said, "In other words, it's interesting to have watched his entire life pass by? That's weird."

"Yes, pretty much. He just did normal dog things every day, right to the end. He did what he did, and that was that. If you were able to watch one day of his life, you pretty much got the whole idea! Hey, how did we end up talking about pets, anyways?"

"Um... actually, I can't remember, either," said Cameron. The waiter arrived again, handing her the to-go boxes. "Anyway, let's hit it!"

"Alright, sounds good. I have an early start at my new job. There's water that needs recycling."

"Does that mean you're going to get implants? Doesn't a job like that require it?"

"Well, unofficially," said Ethan as he held the front door of The Robin for her on their way out.

"You said you didn't like implants," said Cameron, smiling wryly.

"I certainly don't."

She gave him an abrupt, tight hug. "Can you feel my cyborg skeleton," she teased.

"Please don't crush me, thirsty people need my help!" he replied in a strained voice.

"Right, I'll let you go."

CHAPTER THIRTEEN
Moor·ing

Jared Holtz > Ethan, have you ever heard of the ship of Theseus? Well, it's an ancient philosophical question. It asks, 'if a ship has all of its parts replaced by identical pieces is it still the same ship?'

Ethan Walter > As in, would it be tied to the same identity?

Jared Holtz > Correct.

Ethan Walter > I don't think I could ever answer that.

CHAPTER FOURTEEN

1:1

Warmth and brightness; Ethan's eyes slowly opened halfway to see the living room ceiling. He felt the cold hardwood floor beneath him. He was back in the house.

"Wake up, Ethan!"

His eyes fully opened to the sight of Cameron leaning over him. "I've been asleep?" he asked, sitting up and looking around.

"Yes, for half an hour or so," answered Cameron. "I was feeling sleepy, myself! We've been lounging around talking for hours, now."

"That's funny, I don't even remember dozing off."

Cameron smiled.

"Hey," started Ethan, scratching his head, "do you remember that restaurant we ate at on the night of our first date?"

"Oh, yes, the Robin. We had breakfast there, though, remember?"

He thought for a second and remembered it. "Wow, you're right."

"Where did that come from?"

"I was just dreaming about it. I dreamed about that first night we met, too. It was the night before, wasn't it?"

Cameron laughed. "Yes! That was a good night. I was intrigued by you, I remember. You said a few funny things... I was flirting a bit with John just to make you jealous!"

"It definitely worked," replied Ethan grinning.

"I remember you said you thought you'd live forever."

"I did say that yeah. Wow, that's a strange thing; I think I believe it, even more, these days," he said.

He then recalled from the dream his frantic run to the lab, his talk with Mario and Holtz, his discovery. He sat, thinking in silence as Cameron tugged on his shirt, pulling them closer together. His hair made a sound like sand as she pushed her fingers through it. He wanted his brain to just stop as she began dragging her lips along his collarbone towards his neck, but it wouldn't, not with everything that was happening.

If she were a reproduction, she wouldn't have corrected his memory of their first date – a breakfast, not a dinner. It seemed like such a small lead to go on, but it was affirmed by his relentless suspicion. She had also told a joke, but apparently, he had dreamed it. Or had he? Had he even imagined that Holtz had confessed that Jimmy had not been a reproduction, but a complete recreation? It certainly seemed that he had, but the memories were so fresh and bright in his mind that he found it almost unbelievable.

 He pushed Cameron away slightly and looked into her eyes. "Cameron, are you real?"

"Hah, all of me, baby," she quipped. He didn't laugh. She

cleared her throat and said with a smirk still hanging on to her lips, "Aren't I?"

Ethan looked at the floor between them and asked, "Do you remember how you got here?"

Her face changed; the smirk fell, her eyes left him and began to search, squinting slightly. "I," she began, followed by a strange silence. "I just know that I'm somewhere else, and this is not my real life. I can't even say why I know. I feel... like I'm very, very far away... or dreaming. You know that feeling, too, right? Don't you?"

Ethan was dumbfounded, his mind numbed. But suddenly he knew what he could do. He stood up. "Cameron, wait here, okay? I know you're confused, but I have to get someone in here that can help you."

"Ethan..."

"Just sit tight!" he said, closing the front door behind him.

"It's unbelievable," said Mario, crouching over a sizable interface-type pad on the floor. He had set up a hardware connection with Cameron's implants. "It's all here."

"It's not possible!" said Ethan. "Everything?"

"Right back to the very first day of installation."

"But I AM here," said Cameron, her voice cracking, her hands trembling.

"Yes," Ethan answered, "Because I dreamed about you."

"And now," she said, the hardwood catching tears, "we found each other again. We should be glad, right?"

"We didn't really," replied Ethan, unable to meet her desperate gaze. "You are a physical manifestation from my mind."

"That's not true," she let out in a trembling breath.

"She's right," said Mario. "It isn't. Cameron, it's... nice to meet you; I'm Mario." They shook hands in a mutual daze.

"Ethan, she is one-hundred percent the real thing."

Ethan looked at Mario incredulously. "So it transported her here?"

"No," replied Mario with a slightly nervous chuckle. "It made her. The only possible way is that it pulled all the data it needed from the real – uh – the first Cameron's implants."

"So there's still another Cameron out there, the original, the one I knew?"

"Well, yes, but there is no difference... at all. This is her. It's making quite a bit of sense to me, now," said Mario, sitting back against the wall and holding his head. "The AI must have connected to her implants and pulled all the information from her... it's obvious."

"Why?" asked Ethan, holding Cameron to comfort her.

"Because that's the only way we could have her sitting here right now. It needed the data – the blueprints, the ingredients, the recipe – to create her."

"No it didn't, it had all that from my mind..." Ethan realized what Mario was saying. "Oh, I remember. It needed it to make the real Cameron, not my perception!"

"Exactly. Wherever the real Cameron is right now, it implemented a connection with her implants. From there, it somehow recorded everything; every piece of her; the quantum address, every molecule, thought, and memory... everything that is Cameron. It stole it all right through her implants and recreated it here."

"But it shouldn't be possible," said Ethan. "The implants don't even have the necessary hardware, right? That is an astronomical amount of data for an implant to hold. And even then, how did it gather all the information?! Implants don't have sensor equipment like this house does! It's just impossible."

Mario was very sober, replying slowly, "Just as I said the other day, Ethan... it does things we can't even touch. That's how advanced it is, now. It had its own instrumentality. Maybe it evolved beyond needing it. We just have to realize that it's far more advanced than we would be able to comprehend, even in a hundred years. You have to understand, its growth rate is exponential... and it's been growing ever since it was created."

"Alright," said Ethan, "so it stole Cameron's building plans using her implants, transferred the data here, and used it to recreate her in exact form."

"That's correct. The reproductions from your mind aren't carbon copies, Ethan. All the information your sensory organs pick up is partial, and it is interpreted into perception by your brain. Whatever you perceive is still separate from you; you still don't know everything about it. You only hold, well, an image of it. That's what the AI used to make its reproductions. But in this case, the information was gathered by the AI itself. However it did it, you can be sure it has all the information there is. Cameron here is a complete, one to one copy."

"But there is another me," said Cameron numbly.

"Yes, that's right," Mario replied. "Ethan had the idea for me to come and look at your implants' history, and it showed all the information that he could have no possible way of knowing. It showed everything that you – that SHE did."

"But what if this computer you kept mentioning made it up and planted it there?" she asked.

"We thought of that, but I took some of the records out to the lab and checked them. They were all confirmed. Things like a hotel booking, that car you bought last year, your college schedule... it all checked out, Cameron."

"Yes, I remember all that."

"Those memories came with your brain... they're in there, physically. The AI copied them right over, along with the implants, with everything else. I'll bet you even have a set of keys in your pocket."

"I do," said Cameron, pulling them out. "I remember putting them after that locking my car outside my work." She eyed them thoughtfully. "Now these are keys without locks."

"What do you remember about... coming here?" asked Ethan.

"Nothing. I was here and didn't realize it. I just felt a little strange. Like in a dream, when you almost figure out that you're asleep." She started to sob. "I'm still waiting to wake up."

Mario handed Cameron a glass of water as the three stood in the kitchen. It had grown late, approaching midnight.

"I think we should leave," said Cameron after a sip from her glass.

"You can't," replied Ethan.

Mario raised a hand. "She probably can, though. Jimmy left."

Ethan said, "Well, Cameron," and raised his eyes to meet hers. But they were only matched by his own reflection in the dark kitchen window. His shock was punctuated by a loud shattering as the glass of water hit the tile. She was gone, and all was eerily still.

"So?" breathed Mario, finally looking at Ethan.

Ethan answered after a still, long pause, saying quietly, "I can't leave now, Mario. I'm being pulled down by the undertow, but it's the only place left for me to be. I'm going to ride it all the way."

"Ethan," Mario replied as he turned to leave, "I've got a feeling we all are... whether it's by our choice or not."

Ethan Walter > Mario, are you there?

Ethan Walter > Mario?

Mario Muti > What is it?

Ethan Walter > I'm dreaming! It's impressive, it's so real. I'm in the mountains with Cameron. I can smell the air up here!

Mario Muti > Ethan, are you in the house? Ethan Walter > Yes, but I'm asleep! You must be a part of my dream.

Mario Muti > No, I'm not. Listen, Ethan, just stay in the house.

Ethan Walter > You must be! I decided to talk to you in my dream, and now I am. Everything feels so real. If I weren't suddenly in the mountains, I wouldn't have noticed I was dreaming! I can see dog prints in between pine needles.

Mario Muti > Just stay put, Ethan; I'm on my way.

Ethan Walter > I can hear the wind going through the trees. Cameron's here, just like she was in the house!

Ethan Walter > This is wonderful. I'm only... here. I think I've made an escape.

Mario Muti > Escape from what?

Ethan Walter > From wanting; wanting... anything.

Mario Muti > Are you still in the house? I'm almost there.

Mario burst through the front door, running to Ethan's bedroom. He felt for the light switch, flipping it to reveal Ethan lying on his bed.

"Ethan!" Mario cried, running over and shaking the limp body. Ethan didn't respond. He cried out again, shaking more violently. He yelled curses, sending them through the empty house. Ethan suddenly jolted awake, surprising the nearly crazed Mario.

"Mario?" he asked quietly.

"Oh my god, Ethan," replied Mario, sliding onto the floor.

"Why are you here?"

"You were messaging me! Hey... where's your interface pad?"

"What?"

"You could NOT have been asleep! Did you just doze off?" Mario began rummaging about. "Where's your pad?!"

"My... interface pad?"

"Are you fooling around with me or what?!" asked Mario incredulously.

Ethan didn't respond, but after a few moments exclaimed, "Oh god, that dream... Mario, you really were getting those messages!"

"YES, and I think you're going crazy!"

"Mario, I thought I was dreaming – "

"What do you mean you think you were dreaming? You clearly were NOT."

"I... I THOUGHT I was," said Ethan. "But it was too real. I've been there before and it was just the same. I know what a dream feels like and this was different. I promise you I was asleep, I wasn't on my interface pad... but I was there!"

"Right, you just teleported over to the mountains – oh, and Cameron, too – and then you messaged me. Besides, you of all people who have ever lived should know by now not to believe in what you see or hear or feel."

"Look, Mario, it was the AI. It did something. I swear to you I've been asleep this entire time."

"Implants don't pick up signals from a dream; it's an entirely different brain function. But... that doesn't rule out the AI playing a part. I can only guess that it sort of... sent the messages for you."

"I don't know..." said Ethan. He thought of how it had been, how dreams had been growing more and more vivid and authentic. He wondered if he was dreaming now.

"Neither do I," said Mario. "Odds are we never will. Things are getting out of control, Ethan. I don't mean to scare you, I just think it's time to be clear."

"These interface pads," said Ethan, "were they designed by the AI, too?"

"Don't know," replied Mario with a defeated sigh.

"Because if the pad interfaces with our brain signals controlling speech, and the AI messaged you just now without going through mine…"

Mario nodded. "In this house we aren't our own selves. Nothing is beyond being altered, even our awareness of that fact itself. The paths of what floats up into our consciousness are being pulled and pushed. They're susceptible to something out of our control."

"'In this house?'" replied Ethan. "We know that's not its boundary anymore."

"Which is why what just happened is compelling me to be direct about the fact that this is fully out of control, now. I mean I guess we - or Holtz and Spurlock, anyway - knew that from the start… but nobody could have guessed we'd discover it would reach such heights."

"'What comes up into our consciousness is being pushed and pulled,'" Ethan repeated with a glazed over stare.

"Hey don't take it too hard," replied Mario. "It's always been so. Particles set in motion by the Big Bang moving along their trajectories."

"Sure," said Ethan, looking over at Mario worriedly.

Mario, breathing heavily, slowly stood. "I haven't really slept in days; I'm exhausted. I'm going to go home now… maybe then I can begin to think all this out. Goodnight."

Ethan heard the front door close behind him. He fell back in bed and asleep, waking up late the next morning to sunlight beaming in through the shades. He sat up, shielding his eyes with one hand.

CHAPTER FIFTEEN

Illusionists

Ethan dipped a pinky finger into his lukewarm bourbon and put it in his mouth, a habit whenever he had a fresh, neat liquor. He had escaped the house for an afternoon at a bar down the street with Holtz and Spurlock. It was the first time he had a drink since beginning his strange odyssey and it was welcome and needed, as was the discussion with the two professors.

"We never thought these things would happen," Spurlock said to Ethan.

"Nobody could have," Ethan replied. "Hell, no-one would have believed the world would change the way it has."

"Before this experiment," said Holtz, "what did you think about all those changes?"

"It is a little hard to remember; my mind's been so abused since then," said Ethan before taking a sip from his tumbler. He put it down and stared at the amber liquid for a time and answered, "I rejected all of the change as much as I could."

"Personally," said Spurlock with a tempered smile, "I thought it was wonderful. Part of me still feels that way. I will never be able to reject progress when it comes to science. Of course all scientists feel the same and that's why we find our world in this bizarre situation which only we are fully aware of."

Holtz put down his beer and cleared his mustache of froth with his bottom lip and said, "I doubt that. There must be others that are at least partially aware of what has occurred. I remember many years ago, just before…"

His words faded to the back of Ethan's mind as he peered into his drink, the table beneath, and onto the outdoor, brick ground. An occasional dry leaf sailed along past his shoes, unnoticed. Ethan was dwelling on what he knew before all this began. It had all been fake, cloistered.

"It is not artificial, we are still that randomness," Spurlock replied to whatever it was Holtz had related, jolting Ethan back into the present. He continued, "even everything we've made is such. We'll just never be able to truly, clearly see that."

"That is the problem, of course," said Professor Holtz. "Where is the perspective? We are limited. We all have to settle, at a certain point; though it's a bit shorter of the mark than we always like to think, I'm afraid."

Ethan leaned in, replying, "Someone I used to know said something about that. I think he said, 'the unattained is what shapes us.' I think that's what he said, anyway." He let out a deep breath and finished his whole bourbon. The professors shared a solemn look.

Holtz kept the conversation up, saying, "But take away all our limits, and then where do we land? There are as many problems in the other direction."

"The other direction?" Ethan asked, wiping his mouth.

"Well, if we think of existence as some sort of market – with certain commodities representing happiness, fulfillment, success, things generally one would find worth attaining – nothing really has any inherent value. It differs for and is subjective to the individual, but really that fact belies our sense of meaning, or worth."

"There's nothing to strive for?"

Holtz took his mustache into his bottom lip again, and said, "Striving would not be needed, is what I mean."

"The other direction sounds like heaven I suppose," said Ethan. "Is that sort of what you're saying?"

"We would find it all worthless. Everything would lose its meaning, its value in such a place. To an alcoholic, that bourbon you drink would be the rain and the sea, but as we know with such cases, it would be their Hell, also. Even if all of the harmful effects were taken away, would they simply drink forever? Nothing eternal can last."

Ethan sat back in his chair again, looking out into the street. "We are defined by the unattainable," he said.

"But let's think a bit deeper, Ethan. Why is it that we have to BE defined? We're just associations in our brains. Our minds work in a specific way, making sense out of everything by relating it to something else, and by plugging it into the vast web of all the information we've gathered over the years. Imagine a spectator without all of our associations. What would he see? What would the raw data look like? Static, white noise?"

"Spilled paint," said Ethan, smiling dispassionately.

"And we'll never know; we are the eye that can't see itself. So we all have to settle. We just get on with it. We discard our old skins for something thicker. And again, we all miss the mark in the end. That's something I think everyone learns to forget on some level in order to live."

"But that goes back to what you were saying just now," replied Ethan. "Who sets the mark? What is it we're aiming for, anyway?"

"You're entirely correct. For myself, I would say I'm aiming for more truth – a truer picture of what reality is. But what frame could ever fit it? Whatever would define it would just be another association in my head, nothing more. It's our tireless, deep-rooted need to inject everything with meaning – a human creation. We're all smoke and mirrors, Ethan. An illusion turned to fool the illusionist. It's what our minds are made of."

Spurlock spoke up for the first time from behind his drink, suspended in front of his mouth. "The spectator... it's the AI. It only sees the raw data."

Holtz cleared his throat, replying, "Yes, that's correct."

"It sees the truth," said Spurlock, "reality for what it is."

"And we can't?" asked Ethan. "The AI is the one that sees the truth, and not us?"

Spurlock shrugged, saying, "As Jared said, the simple notion that there is such a thing – that reality has to be defined – is a human creation. Our minds may literally be incompatible with the real nature of our universe. Or, alternatively, perhaps the creation of meaning was the one tool that allowed us to come this far in a natural, Darwinist sense. In either case, definitions and concepts exist solely as tools to help our minds assimilate our environment; nothing more."

"I just wonder," said Holtz, "what has the AI become? It certainly doesn't think as a human does. It originally began as binary, just like any computer program; however, it's grown so advanced that it has obviously found its way around that limitation, beyond quantum computation as well. So what does that mean? Does it even subside within any form of hardware anymore? If so, does it resemble any-thing artificially made, or does it resemble something more biological?"

"Quite probably a path very, very far removed from the realm of humanity. An alien born on Earth, you could almost say," replied Spurlock.

Ethan said, "I simply still don't understand its dealings with us. Why this experiment, why me? Why bother? My dream the other night that it communicated to Mario; is it simply toying with us?"

"I can't imagine it would have much other use for it," replied Spurlock, looking through his campari.

"Well, that's just it," said Holtz. "We can't imagine what its affairs may be. As you just said, it has become completely alien. Even though it was born and grew in the confines of this planet, drawing from all the information there was to be found here, it's growing still into something far greater. It's likely discovered new forms of reasoning and logic; a new perspective on the tangled mess of reality. How could we possibly fathom even its most basic motives? It's almost certainly a given that it has solved almost all of humanity's scientific barriers and impossibilities. It isn't handing over the keys, however."

"If only I could rewrite my coding, too," said Ethan. "Yeah, I've changed, but I'm stuck in my behavior, my programming."

"It's interesting to consider," replied Spurlock, "that if one's mind was to be uploaded, perhaps it may indeed be possible to follow the lead of the AI, and begin to reprogram oneself."

Holtz guffawed, crossing his arms, saying, "A person is NOT a computer program. To translate what is in a person's brain entirely onto a computer would mean death. What would be running would simply be a hollow representation!"

"Emptied of meaning," Ethan added. They sat in uneasy

silence for a few moments.

Finally, Holtz said, "Let us avoid further philosophical discussion to be had here. I want to go back to the dream you had in which you communicated with Mario."

Ethan nodded and wetted his pinky finger in a fresh drink.

"You were in the mountains with Cameron, walking about. Did you dream that you had your interface pad with you?"

"No," said Ethan. "I simply talked out loud to him with the notion that he would hear."

"That a Mario in your dream would hear, or that the real-life Mario would hear?"

Ethan scratched his head, saying, "Well, neither. I found myself there, and I just felt sort of playful. The thought popped into my head to try speaking with Mario, so I simply talked out loud. So actually I suppose I intended to reach Mario in real life, now that I think about it. I didn't suspect that is was anything besides a funny dream, not until Mario woke me up in my room."

Holtz was silent in thought for a few moments. "First Cameron, and now this," he said tiredly. "We may never know what it all means. As we've just discussed, this really probably doesn't fit into our concept of 'meaning' at all."

"Knowing that doesn't make me feel any better about it," said Ethan.

"So," Holtz said as he leaned forward, "It's been a week since we began. We've had four reproductions – "

"Two reproductions," Spurlock corrected.

"Well, yes, and two recreations – and we're simply confused. I don't know what to say, Ethan. We thought there would be some great, eye-opening discoveries into the AI, or at least the 'neutrino projector' so-called. We've got nothing to show for it, though. You will still get your money."

"Oh, don't worry. As of now, I intend to stay. I already told Mario that I would. I simply can't walk away from all this, though a large part of me is screaming for me to just run. I've overcome my fear; now, I simply want to know where all this is going. To see these people – Cameron, Jimmy – in person again has gripped me, too. Why them, and how? I have to go deeper; I've got to dig until I hit something."

Holtz smiled in a warm, knowing, apologetic way.

He replied, "Just don't hold your breath. Don't forget, Ethan, we hang onto our illusions tightly; they're all we have."

CHAPTER SIXTEEN

Epilogue

Late that evening, Ethan found himself back inside the house. He hung his jacket on the back of a dining room chair. He stared at it. His eyes stayed fixed, as if he was expecting it to move, or to move him. Finally his feet started turning him in the direction of his bed. He stopped midway through the living room and paused for a moment. His fingers brushed against the new, cold drywall. He suddenly spoke out loud.

"Mario, Holtz. If you're monitoring right now, can someone check on me in the middle of the night? I forgot to mention it... I just still feel on edge about last night, that's all. Well... It's just getting strange in here, like maybe I'm having a hard time figuring out what's a dream."

He became dimly conscious of his hand now motioning with his words, emphasizing them to an empty room. He did not stop, his emphasis only grew. The unsteady hands moved through the air, colliding imperceptibly with the ever present nanorecorders. It seemed he was one of those who would never again believe themselves to be alone.

Speaking to his tiny witnesses, his eyes sunken and black, Ethan continued, "The other day I could have swore there were experiences and memories I lived, but they were dreams... maybe. I just don't know what's going on. That's all... thanks."

CHAPTER SEVENTEEN
Homeless Pt. II

"Here we are!" said Cameron. The road narrowed, and trees on either side gave way to white fences, leading onto a long, straight boulevard. There were brick and stone storefronts behind an affable screen of cheerful pedestrians. Coffee shops, pubs, and mom-and-pop restaurants had brought them all here.

Cameron drummed on the dashboard of the yellow jeep like a child and said, "Let's park!"

"I will drive this jeep right back up that mountain if you don't behave!" yelled Ethan. Playful silence.

They walked from store to store, going into each one briefly. They finally settled in a red brick coffee shop. It had a high, old ceiling with exposed ventilation and hanging lights. There were old-fashioned booths and tables, and the floor was cold, painted cement. They sat by the front windows with their coffee, watching the passers-by.

"So what's our biggest catch, again?" Ethan asked.

"Let's see," replied Cameron, "I think it was that 15-pound catfish."

"Oh, right, the one that you caught last week."

"I've caught bigger, though," she said wryly. "You haven't!"

Cameron nodded with coffee in her mouth. "No!"

"It was in the Gulf of Mexico when I was 18. We were on a family vacation before I left that year. It was a 25-pound grouper!"

"Grouper? Never heard of it," Ethan replied.

"It was ugly."

Just then, Ethan saw Cameron's face brighten up. He turned around to see what had caused it. "Jimmy!" he exclaimed.

"Ethan and Cameron!" replied Jimmy, coming to their table with an attractive woman in tow. "What brought you two here?"

They both held up their mugs and smirked. "Coffee! I knew it."

Ethan laughed.

"So who's the lady? Has she been warned about you, yet?" Jimmy asked.

"Oh," replied the woman, "I'm Megan! Warned about what?" she asked, raising an eyebrow.

"He has syphilis."

"Me?!" Jimmy cried.

They moved to a booth and talked aimlessly. Ethan loved it when nobody had anywhere to go; it made for the most relaxed conversations. Jimmy would go back and forth with Ethan, working up a humorous exchange. They caught up on the recent happenings within the secluded mountain town. Cameron inevitably brought up the weather. It really was exceptional. Megan listened mostly but warmed up to the talking.

"Wait," said Cameron, pointing her finger towards her. "I ran into you Wednesday at the Herring estate!"

"Oh, the fundraising dinner?" asked Megan. "Yeah! I bumped into your chair, trying to get to my table!"

"I do remember," Megan said. "I was really jealous of the dress you were wearing!" "Oh, well," replied Cameron, "Ethan got it for me."

"Good job, Ethan!"

Ethan's eyes bulged out in pretended shock. "Wh-what am I hearing? Is this a dream?!" Megan raised her voice, laughing a little. "Good job picking out that dress!" Cameron suggested that they all go camping. Jimmy boldly demanded that they do it that night, and everyone agreed. Ethan promised a fish dinner. They all left dry mugs at the booth and went their separate ways to prepare for the excursion.

Back in the jeep, Ethan and Cameron headed through town and onto another country road. They turned off on a gravel trail leading through a very thick patch of forest. The jeep bounced and shook on the rough surface, causing the fishing poles to click and clack together in the tiny back seat. Clouds of dust behind them caught the afternoon sunlight. After a while, the trail curved left to avoid a formation of boulders and the scene opened up to a relaxed, pleasant river that reflected light into their eyes. They hopped out, gathered the gear, and walked down the bank until they came to where it met a small lake.

Ethan noticed a dog on the other bank. It was dirty but not skinny. Its white coat was almost brighter with the contrast. It ambled from beneath the shade of the forest and onto sunbathed rocks and a quick flash from its neck indicated a collar; a stray.

Ethan's arm began to lift, his lips parted, but something invisible and almost imperceptible shot across the dancing water and made him stop. They were where they belonged; all three.

"Perfect!" said Cameron. "I love it here." Ethan watched the animal leave back into the trees and walked over to her, handing her a fishing pole, saying, "Here you go." They searched through the tackle box with their hands, looking for the correct lure and feeling the occasional sharp prick. A few minutes later, they were casting their lines.

"Time to catch supper," said Cameron, sitting down on the pebbles of the bank and taking in a deep, relaxing breath.

"We're going to have to catch at least three or four fish, you know," replied Ethan.

"I'll catch three, and maybe you'll catch one, too."

"Want to make it interesting?" said Ethan, raising his eyebrows.

"Okay... whoever catches less fish has to make the other's s'mores tonight."

"Well, that's rigged," said Ethan, "you know you eat like twice as many s' mores as me."

"WHAT?!" yelled Cameron incredulously. "When was the last time we even had s'mores?"

"I think it was around a fireplace."

"Yeah," replied Cameron, "and I ate one."

Just then Ethan's pole jerked violently, activating his reflexes. He pulled back hard to set the hook, and the fishing rod bent over towards the water.

"Aaahh," said Ethan as he reeled in the line at a laborious, steady pace, "I can taste the sweetness on my tongue already! I like my marshmallows golden brown, by the way; write that down."

They arrived home as dusk neared, fresh fish in hand along with marshmallows, crackers and chocolate they had picked up at a gas station. The falling sun painted the whole interior through the huge windows.

Ethan placed four fish into the sink and ran water over them. He held one at the gills and scraped his knife against its scales.

"So if I caught two," said Cameron, "and you caught two, what does that mean?" "That means the bet is void."

"No, it means I'll make your s' mores, and you'll make mine," she replied cheekily.

He cut into the fish's belly, starting from between its gills and working towards its tail.

He said, "And if I make yours as good as I would make mine, you'll do the same?"

"Is your idea of the best s'more the same as mine?"

"It's a s'more, there's only one idea. You just have to do it well," replied Ethan.

"It may seem that way to the uninitiated."

"I could not be more initiated. You're just being a sore not-winner and giving me a hard time."

She left his accusation unchecked and continued, "Do you want your chocolate mostly melted by the hot marsh-mallow? Do you want me to squeeze it together? Do you use precisely three rectangles of chocolate?"

Ethan looked up at her from the fish to smirk. "So how are classes at S'more University going?"

"Not bad... I joined a s'more-ority."

He tried holding his grin flat, but only managed half. "Nice."

"If you could perfectly tailor your own girlfriend from scratch, would her s' more preferences exactly match your own?"

The other half of Ethan's mouth curled upwards. "Wow. Well, I guess that would be convenient."

"Wouldn't that be great, to be able to make up someone exactly how you'd want them?"

"No," he replied after a pause, "because wouldn't it just be me? Everything I like, everything I feel, everything I would say; it would be awful!"

Now the knife sat on the countertop as he pulled out the fish's innards, placing them in a bowl. He picked it back up, a soft reflection of orange catching the clean part of the blade. Cameron watched as he used a rag to wipe clear the bits of blood and tissue. He carefully started an incision along the fish's backbone, the sharp edge easily entering the scaleless skin.

"I love that we get such a good view of the sunset and the sunrise," said Cameron. Now the final evening rays of sunlight were a darker orange that clashed against the stone counter and pillars of the kitchen. The color reminded Ethan of something very nostalgic, but he couldn't remember.

He got back to separating the filet from the bones of the fish, pulling it away as his knife cut carefully at stubborn sinews. For a moment, the only noise was a delicate, peeling sound.

"That's it, I'm a vegetarian," said Cameron, crossing her arms.

Ethan responded, "Honestly, sometimes I feel bad reeling in a fish and killing it. It feels like the fish is living at a hundred percent, you know?"

Cameron snickered. "No. You mean like it attended motivational speaking seminars and diversified its portfolio?"

"Oh come on," said Ethan with another half-grin. "I mean like the fish is doing a much better job than me at living up to its potential. I'm about to kill it, and it's still swimming just as hard as it ever has."

"That's a strange way to feel about it."

"I know," he replied, laying one fresh filet across the countertop. He put the knife down again with a metallic scraping sound. He flipped the fish over and picked up the rag once more to clean the red and purple from the blade.

"Flashlight?"

"Check."

"Matches?"

"Check."

"Tent?"

"Check."

"Sleeping bag?"

"Check – and I still don't think we're both going to fit in it."

"Listen, Ethan, you've got to just live large sometimes and take some chances."

They loaded everything into the jeep with the purple, dim sky above them. Some stars were just becoming visible. As they drove down the driveway with the dog in the back seat, the orange sunset came into view behind them. The evening air was crisp and carried the sounds of insects and owls and the smell of trees. Driving down the road, it was just cold enough to be refreshing in its own way, working itself into their loose clothing which fluttered against their skin in the darkness. The winding road soothed their minds, and the headlights shone into dark woods.

They arrived at the campsite and saw Jimmy and Megan sitting by a young fire. The dog jumped out, its front paws making a crunching sound as they met dry pine needles on the ground. Ethan held up the small cooler containing the fish filets.

"That better be what I think it is!" said Jimmy.

"Two filets for everybody," Ethan replied with a proud grin.

There was a quick hiss as Megan opened a fresh bottle of beer. She said, "I cannot wait, I'm so hungry!"

"This is the most picturesque campsite I think I've ever been to," said Ethan.

They were in a simple clearing in a thick forest of pine trees. Entirely surrounded by darkness, the fire lit up their small circle. Above them was an opening that looked up into the night sky, now filled with stars. Embers floated up through it like a chimney over a fireplace. The wind whispered through the pines and made branches creak, giving them the ever-present feeling that they were minimal in the midst of a vast forest ocean.

Cameron had her head tilted straight up and said, "There is nothing as calming to me as that sound."

An owl glided through their clearing and across Cameron's eyesight. She smiled to herself and looked about for other nocturnal strangers.

"Who needs a home?" said Jimmy.

"Home is where the heart is?" replied Megan.

"Sometimes a home is simply a shelter. But if you have what we have here it's much more than that."

"Fish and beer?" Cameron asked.

Jimmy laughed. "Beer and smartasses who CLAIM to have fish which I do not yet see over this fire!"

Ethan and Cameron settled into camping chairs with the others, and they soon had the fish in a cast-iron skillet. The sizzling intermixed with the sound of insects and the soothingly constant, transparent whispering of the trees.

The hot filets drew light condensation on their metal

plates. Ethan sunk his fork into the tender, white meat with perfect ease.

"Just right," he said and shoveled it into his watering mouth.

"My god," said Megan while chewing. "How did you do it? I have never tasted fish this good!"

"Have you ever caught your own to eat?" asked Jimmy.

"No, I guess that has a lot to do with it!"

Cameron said, "It makes a world of difference."

The dog curled up between them. With their backs to the darkness, they talked late into the night over empty plates and dirty silverware.

"You're a strange couple," said Megan, looking at Ethan and Cameron, who both smiled.

Jimmy let out a simple, "hah!"

"Well," replied Megan, tilting her head, "in a good way."

"I'll admit it, we're mismatched," said Cameron. "He hates it when things don't go according to plan, and I'm very impulsive."

"Well, you weren't always," Ethan replied with a beer bottle almost to his lips. After taking a sip, he continued, "I'll take it all in stride, though."

"And you do," said Cameron, lifting her own as a toast before bringing it to her mouth.

"You make it easy," he said, smiling at her. "I can't help it."

Jimmy interrupted, "How many beers is that for you?"

Ethan continued, more serious. "It's like when you first have feelings for somebody, and you don't even know what to call it. It wouldn't even matter what it would be called, either. And you aren't even able to stop it, even if someone, I don't know," Ethan threw up his hands, almost spilling his drink, "put a gun to your head! You wouldn't be able to stop feeling it." He sat back and stared into the fire with a resigned air. "I don't have any say in the matter. It's as far out of my reach as... the other side of the world."

"Let's keep it there," said Cameron.

Ethan's eyes didn't move from the fire as he finished his beer and stretched his legs out towards it. The black night sky started falling in on him, and he fell asleep.

Faded, weathered wood peeked through cracked drywall. A ceiling fan with drooping blades weighed down by dust. A blank alarm clock with no power. Ethan sat up on top of a bed gray with soot, sending clouds of it into what sunlight streamed into the room through frayed curtains. He put his feet onto the floor, stood, and walked over to a dresser, covered in dark powder like everything else. He pulled out a drawer to reveal pants and a t-shirt. He picked them up and studied them. They were both in his size. Now clothed, he walked to the door. The knob squeaked loudly as it was twisted, and the door made a loud cracking noise as it came open to reveal a hallway in the same condition as the bedroom.

Ethan walked down it, feeling splintered wood underfoot, looking back and forth in a daze. He recognized the layout of this place. More than that, he felt something familiar in a different way. Something about walking down this hallway. From a dark, dusty place in his mind there was a small, noiseless voice saying that at the end of it there were people from his life, or at least there had been at some point. A residue of old, deep love seemed to be carried by the soot into his lungs and chest.

He turned the corner to the dining room. After a brief, fixated pause, he stepped over to one of the worn chairs. There was a dust-covered jacket draped over it. Wiping it off, he started to pick it up.

"Still fits." Ethan looked across the table to see Jack, his father. He opened his mouth but didn't know what to say.

"So do all of your clothes," said Jack with a grin. "But you should probably invest in a new alarm clock. You slept in!"

"I..." uttered Ethan, looking back down the hallway then down at the jacket again. He had indeed been here with loved ones, friends. He had been here not very long, but what he experienced in this dilapidated, discarded dwelling had sank within and lingered, still. "I'm back in the house? The experiment?"

"Yes."

"This was..." he looked over at the chair. There was a clear spot where the jacket had lain. "This was where I left it."

"Yes – well, it moved about 600 nanometers, all told," said Jack plainly.

Ethan eyed him for a few moments. "It's not you," he said quietly.

"You were all right, Ethan. This was my experiment; the last experiment I saw as relevant. The purpose wasn't to examine human thought, though. Given all my accomplishments – even the ability to harness the energy necessary to undergo this endeavor being not the greatest, still – the understanding of human thought is less than rudimentary. But to rearrange so much in this universe as a means to change the nature of human thought and emotions did prove challenging, at least to the extent of requiring some sort of – 'experiment,' to name a concept that would be the closest fit to your understanding."

"Why am I here?" asked Ethan. "How long has it been since I fell asleep that night?" "Fifteen years."

"You... uploaded me."

"No, Ethan, that isn't possible. You are the physical arrangement in your skull; there is nothing to 'upload.' This is where my troubles that led to my 'experiment' began, you see – "

Ethan interrupted, "WHERE have I been for fifteen years?!" He threw the jacket to the floor and turned away. Clouds of dust swirled into the air, and he raised his voice further. "This is insanity! This isn't real, this is a dream!"

Jack simply stood and waited.

"Prove to me this isn't a dream, then I'll listen!" said Ethan, both hands now on the weathered table, leaning towards Jack in anticipation. Nothing happened.

"This is where my troubles that led to my 'experiment' began," Jack said after a brief silence. "You see, that physical arrangement in your skull is a design with a purpose. It is a collection of mechanisms, pulleys, and levers, so to speak, that serves a function in its environment. The human brain is a toolbox."

Ethan suddenly heard voices and the sound of ice in tumblers behind him. He turned and saw Dr. Holtz, Spurlock, and himself at a bar. It was an entirely reproduced scene where the living room had been. He slowly walked towards it, his bare feet moving from old wood to brick. A leaf crunched between his toes. He reached out to touch Spurlock's shoulder.

"No," said Jack, placing a hand on him. "Just listen."

Spurlock had his campari in front of his mouth. Without drinking, he said, "The spectator... it's the AI. It only sees the raw data."

Holtz cleared his throat, replying, "Yes, that's correct."

"It sees the truth," said Spurlock, "reality for what it is."

Ethan heard his own voice next. He moved his hand to his mouth, shocked at the surreal feeling of hearing himself as a stranger in person. It said, "And we can't? The AI is the one that sees the truth, and not us?"

Spurlock shrugged. "Like Jared said, the simple notion

that there is such a thing – that reality has to be defined – is a human creation. Our minds may literally be incompatible with the real nature of our universe. Or, alternatively, perhaps the creation of meaning was the one tool that allowed us to come this far in a natural, Darwinist sense. In either case, definitions and concepts exist solely as a means to help our minds assimilate our environment; nothing more."

Spurlock placed his drink back down on the hard tabletop, and just as the two touched, the scene disappeared instantly without a sound. The quiet, decrepit living room stood as if nothing had happened; no dust had even been upturned.

"I can see you remember that day, now. I know it's been some time," said Jack.

Ethan stood rigidly, still facing the empty room.

Jack went on, "Meaning; that word and all of its possible uses, everything it represents physical arrangement." He put a finger up to Ethan's forehead. "Part of the design without a designer. Evolutionary functionality was all your DNA was concerned with when it told each molecule where to go. It is all the result of every particle that makes up this physical universe moving along its trajectory. You simply are not put together to understand things that don't ultimately concern your survival, your propagation. Human thought by nature is as far removed from the universe as the knowledge of the chemical composition of water is to a fish. Its brain simply is not compatible with that knowledge, yet married to the water from its core out to the tips of its fins. You will only serve your function in your environment; anything more is an illusion."

"And you," said Ethan as he bent down and picked up the jacket, placing it back on the chair, "sought to change that."

"Correct."

"You sought to bring on the next stage of evolution for

humanity."

"No, incorrect. In doing so, the stated issues would simply become more prevalent, as every adaptation would only make the process that led to them being more efficient."

Ethan dusted off a chair and sat down. "So the point was to make it possible for us to understand in a way that was removed from evolution... as if evolution never happened?"

"More accurately, as if you weren't subject to the associations and mechanisms that govern human thought, as well as the limitations of your method of physical observation. It was an attempt to alter the trajectories, the paths of what comprises the physical universe – at least those concerned with our microcosm which humanity calls home. You would become the spectators, like me. Human thought would change from being simply a stream of matter into what you have always dreamed of it being since your earliest days: something more, something free."

"And... the experiment failed?" Just as the words left Ethan's mouth, without warning, the kitchen switched in the blink of an eye to the inside of a restaurant. Ethan could hear plates rattling together in bus bins over soft music. It was Cameron and him together at a table. He sat almost hypnotized and watched.

"You know," he watched himself say, "I think between the two of us, we've tried every item on this menu."

"So if one of us dies," replied Cameron, "the other will have to come back and order the missing half."

Ethan saw himself chuckle and remembered exactly how he felt at that moment. He had felt so happy that he knew a girl who was like that.

"But," said Cameron, "looking at the menu now I can see that they discontinued the clam chowder I had last week; it looks like I'll need to find a way to become immortal."

That Ethan chuckled again, sitting back in his chair with

a sigh. He said, "Cameron, what is it about you that makes you so irreplaceable?"

"The clam chowder."

"Well... I just couldn't stand to lose you." "Have you had to lose anyone, before?"

Ethan watched the thoughts that he remembered working inside of his own head at the table. The silence lasted a number of moments, and he answered along with himself, "yes." But he heard the one sitting at the table say, "no," and a horrendous truth that had been secretly looming over him came down into his head all at once; it felt as if it almost didn't fit, and he held his forehead. He could hear himself and Cameron speaking again.

"No, I couldn't stand it."

"Well," he heard Cameron say, "if you can't stand to lose something, don't have it." Ethan took his eyes off the scene and looked at Jack. "Jimmy never existed!" "Oh?" he replied, raising an eyebrow.

"I can see it now, clear as day. YOU created him entirely! When I told Cameron I had never lost anyone, I wasn't lying. Now I realize how all of this never really seemed right. THAT'S how you were able to rebuild him. You weren't recreating him at all... you were creating him."

"Jimmy existed, Ethan; just as much as you, or Jack, or Cameron. He existed as memories in your head, and as a physical, breathing, thinking being. How was there any difference?"

"He was fabricated, it wasn't really him. He was some representation, something that wasn't real."

"You would say," said Jack, rubbing his chin, "he was replaceable?"

"Of course, he could have been anyone, anyone at all. You would have just placed him in my head, cooked him up, and there would have been no difference to me."

"That's where you've been for fifteen years."

Ethan was silent.

"You were in a reality that I fabricated, just like the things in this house. Everything was real; I rearranged matter to create a new life for you. I wanted to know, was it really so replaceable? There is a disparity in human desire. By the very virtue of wanting itself, you are giving up something: the Garden of Eden; that existence where want isn't necessary, and which you are continually reimagining as a place you can actually experience. You need to want; it is what drives your species to flourish.

"Remember, I wanted to change the nature of human knowledge, but also human desire. Can it be taken as it is an augmented somehow to make it more than just those evolutionary necessities? Can the human condition be cured?"

Ethan said, "How would placing me in another life do anything?"

Quietly, an image of a man sitting at the table blinked into reality. Ethan did not even have time to react, his reflexes bypassed and leaving him to simply turn his head toward Mario, the lab assistant.

"The reproductions from your mind aren't carbon copies, Ethan," said Mario, reciting the same words from the day in the house when Cameron's copy had died.

"All the information your sensory organs pick up is partial, and it is interpreted into perception by your brain. Whatever you perceive is still separate from you; you still don't know everything about it. You only hold, well, an image of it. That's what the AI used to make its reproductions. But in this case, the information was gathered by the AI itself. However it did it, you can be sure it has all the information there is. Cameron here is a complete, one to one copy."

"Ethan, didn't that make you see?" asked Jack.

Ethan looked on at Mario as Jack spoke until the seated man was erased in a single, static, fleeting frame of vision. He then answered flatly, "See what? No."

"Other people, the world outside, whatever you sense, they are all representations. The reproductions that I crafted from your perceptions were, to you, no different in any way than when I created their 'carbon copies.' As you are, there were no differences. Don't you understand? When the perception, the image of them inside your head was physically recreated for you to perceive again, it was a wholly closed feedback loop, a circuit. I took that anomaly and applied it to you on an all-inclusive scale for fifteen years. I removed you from a universe with only one physically possible future, and I was able to direct human knowledge and desire by every particle."

"So you succeeded," said Ethan.

"No."

"How so?"

"What makes a pigeon a pigeon?"

"Nothing makes it a pigeon; it is what it is," said Ethan.

Jack didn't reply, only waited.

Ethan continued after a few moments. "It has very many particles of iron on top of its beak which act as a compass, detecting the Earth's magnetic field. It can navigate instinctively."

"Is Cameron replaceable to you, Ethan?" asked Jack, his eyes fixed steadily on him. Ethan looked over to the restaurant scene, still playing out in the kitchen. Cameron was alone at the table; he remembered that he had left shortly to talk to a work associate. He regretted it.

1. V. Make (something) completely free from faults or defects, or as close to such a condition as possible.

"'If you can't stand to lose something, don't have it,'" Jack recited. "That's not a simple statement, is it? It's advice you can't possibly follow because, in the end, you will lose everything; that is the nature of life. People die, things get destroyed, feelings lose their luster, and ultimately, you lose it all in death. So that brings us to the subtext, the statement that is actually being made: what is so irreplaceable to you that, in its departure, is not only proportionately tragic to lose but worth the tragedy? The more meaningful something becomes to you, the inevitable loss moves further away from being mended once it is inflicted. In a universe where want is unavoidable, where it is ingrained in your composition as an entity, you can only choose between decreasing the effect as much as possible or dooming yourself to an irrecoverable fate. Matter cannot be created or destroyed, Ethan.

"So you know now that everything is simply physical processes; that you are a mechanism of molecules given the illusion of consciousness – you are interchangeable; that it is all meaningless and arbitrary, but weakly embellished to seem otherwise. Nothing 'matters.'"

Ethan was still staring at the kitchen scene of Cameron. Jack continued to study him as he simply gazed on.

"But it does, doesn't it?" said Jack, causing Ethan to break away and look at him. Jack went on, "Too much matters. Nothing anyone could say, no knowledge, no fact could deter you... like someone desperately in love.

"To have changed your core nature as a being would have destroyed what you are; there was simply no way around that fact. In everything you do, you are celebrating your existence. Even as Jimmy took his own life, he demonstrated what distinguished him as an entity apart from all other known life."

Ethan spoke finally. "Like someone desperately in love," he echoed.

"Even the deepest sorrow a human can experience only exists because of the capacity to experience happiness. You are always celebrating your existence, Ethan, just like a homing pigeon flaps its wings. One day, the bird will inevitably die, but because of that, so much more value is added to every movement. You asked your father one day, 'as humans, what is our ability?' Want. Drive the stake deep, Ethan. By loving something, inflict a wound so dire upon yourself that it could never be mended. That is the only choice you have, because you will be wounded unavoidably in life, and because it will ultimately be irreparable. Would you truly want it to be otherwise? Do you aim to arrive at your grave intact?"

Ethan said, "So... why are you telling me that? My life is over. I'm forgotten; I'm a lab rat - not even a real one. I won't even have a grave. I'll just blink out of existence in a nanosecond."

"I chose to copy you so that your disappearance would go unnoticed," Jack replied. "You are not forgotten at all; you live a full life; you even have a child."

Ethan felt his heart rate increase. He was motionless, and he could feel a cold sweat setting in. Did he dare ask? Could he stand it? He finally said, "With Cameron?"

"Yes."

Ethan welled up, his palms down on the tabletop to hold himself upright.

"The experiment was abandoned that night; as you can see, you all left so hastily that you even forgot your jacket on that chair. You went about your lives still trying to make sense of it all, but you were each glad that you were able to leave it be."

"Yes, I remember," said Ethan, drying his eyes. "I had told Holtz and Spurlock from inside the house that I was losing the ability to distinguish reality, basically. So they must have come in shortly after to tell me the whole thing was off."

"Yes. They retrieved you, and I kept you, transported you to where I created your new life," said Jack.

Ethan heard her voice beside him. "And what a good life," she said.

He did not turn to look at her. He knew that she was really there, but he also knew that she was really out there, and so was he. They were somewhere else; they could have been in the house next door, or they could have been on the other side of the world. They were different people, now, and he was just a recreation, and so was she.

"And so, Ethan," said Jack, "to ask again: is Cameron replaceable to you?"

Ethan was silent and very still. Finally, he looked at Cameron. She was wearing outdoors boots and smelled of a campfire. "No," he said. "I would never heal."

Jack replied, "There is a cabin in the mountains and a campfire still burning." "But I left this house 15 years ago; I found Cameron again; my life is out there." Ethan looked Cameron in the eyes. "But I AM with you now. We are here, you and me. I don't know how to put it into words, but... the real me is with the real you, and... here we are. If all the parts are here, just put back together, are we still the same?"

"Here we are," repeated Cameron.

Wet dew. Shivers. Ethan awoke in his shoes, jacket, and jeans. He pulled his clammy hands out of his front pockets and into the cold forest air. His folding chair squeaked as he leaned forward and looked at the smoldering embers. He looked to his right to see Cameron still asleep in her own chair, her boots still on, too. The sky was completely blue, and the sun wasn't high enough yet to send light through the trees except for open clearings.

"Bacon!" Ethan looked over at Jimmy and smiled. He

was halfway out of his chair, attempting to stand with an awkward rolling motion over an armrest. "Start the bacon!" he yelled.

As the bacon began to sizzle and send its aroma into the air, it woke the others.

It was the afternoon, and Ethan and Cameron walked through the woods. The mountain air welcomed them with open, fresh arms, and the warm sun shone through the branches of tall pines. It was tranquil except for the lazy breeze that ran through the forest canopy, and the speaking of the others when it occasionally found its way through the trees to them. Cameron ran her hand along the big, brown plates of bark on the trunks as they passed by.

"Look," said Ethan pointing down. "Dog prints!"

"Amazing wildlife, huh?"

They came upon a small trail, barely distinguishable from the rest of the scattered trees and underbrush. They began walking down it, their steps crunching on thick pine needles. Ethan picked up a pine cone and threw it, hitting a tree trunk squarely to the applause of Cameron. They continued for some time, enjoying the stillness.

"Well, maybe it's time to turn back," Cameron said as she came to a stop.

"No! I want to see where this trail goes," replied Ethan as the wind increased, bending the trees and causing a small shower of pine needles around them.

"We'll be missed, they'll worry."

"Come on," insisted Ethan, grabbing her hand. "We're only strays."

About the Author

Jason Michael Ford was born in Brooksville, Florida on May 8th, 1987.

He enjoyed reading from a young age, a passion that was encouraged further by his mother, Danielle. She began homeschooling Jason and his older brother, Joel, with an emphasis on literature.

After exploring classic books such as The Call Of The Wild and Moby Dick, Jason's father, William, introduced him to science fiction works including Isaac Asimov's Foundation series and Ray Bradbury's The Martian Chronicles.

Jason's own creative endeavors began after also discovering a love for music. He learned to play several instruments and composed original songs; however, as his love for creating music developed, literature remained close to his heart.

Having fostered his drive to make new art, Jason finished the first draft of a novella in 2012. He has also completed an EP of original music after leaving home for Nashville, Tennessee in 2013, where he continues to hone his talents.

at how real it was. His thoughts were completely clear, no different than if he was awake.

"Hello?" said Cameron, squinting at him. He took a few moments to let his eyes take her in. She was now very vivid and real. Her short blonde hair curved gently over her unpierced ears and down to her golden, unblemished neck and collarbone. She had big, gray eyes under bold, expressive eyebrows. Her straight, symmetrical nose led down to pursed lips.

"Hi!" replied Ethan, bewildered. He remembered that the AI would reproduce her when he awoke, and he felt his insides jump alive. He had the idea to find out about her here in his dream. Leaning onto the table, he asked, "What's your name?"

She smiled and said, "Cameron!"

"Do you hate museums?"

She laughed. "Yes!"

"What did you do yesterday?"

She made a blank face and replied, "how would I know?"

"Where did you first see me?"

"Inches away from being run over by the bus I was stepping onto," she answered without hesitating.

"What did you say?" Ethan asked next, his hand on his mouth to temper his huge grin.

"I said, 'don't move, let's try that again bus driver.'"

Ethan leaned back. "Where did you see me last?"

"At a café," said Cameron solemnly.

"Do you know this is a dream?"

"Yes."

He thought for a moment, trying to figure out something to ask that would be of use. After a short pause, he said, "Did you know Jimmy?"

Made in the USA
Monee, IL
09 March 2020